"Move!"

The car was on top of them. Cara stared at it, paralyzed. At the last second she flung herself into the brush and the car rocketed past.

Cara half lay in the brush, unable to stop trembling. She smelled damp rotting leaves. Nancy was crying a few feet away. "Stupid jerk," Cara yelled.

. . . As she brushed off the knees of her jeans, she heard Nancy cry out, "*Cara!*"

Headlights slammed into her eyes. She screamed and turned. The car veered toward her, thumping over fallen logs. Cara ran wildly as the car pursued her.

Books by Richard Posner

Someone to Die For
Sweet Sixteen and Never Been Killed

Available from ARCHWAY PAPERBACKS

Sweet Sixteen
AND
NEVER BEEN KILLED

Richard Posner

AN ARCHWAY PAPERBACK
Published by POCKET BOOKS
New York   London   Toronto   Sydney   Tokyo   Singapore

This book is a work of fiction. Names, characters, places, and incidents are either products of the author's imagination or are used fictitiously. Any resemblance to actual events or locales or persons, living or dead, is entirely coincidental.

AN ARCHWAY PAPERBACK *ORIGINAL*

An Archway Paperback published by
POCKET BOOKS, a division of Simon & Schuster Inc.
1230 Avenue of the Americas, New York, NY 10020

ISBN: 0-671-86506-4

First Archway Paperback printing September 1993

10 9 8 7 6 5 4 3 2 1

AN ARCHWAY PAPERBACK and colophon
are registered trademarks of Simon & Schuster Inc.

Cover art by Lisa Falkenstern

Printed in the U.S.A.

IL: 7+

To Jarrod, Mark, and Alayna,
my most beloved young adults.

Sweet Sixteen
AND
NEVER BEEN KILLED

CHAPTER

1

*C*ara Nelson, please report to the English book-room. Cara Nelson—"

Cara snatched the pass out of Mr. Graham's hand the second he finished writing it and clattered down the stairs. Arriving at the bookroom, she peered through the glass window. There stood Dyann Wilson, sobbing, with Mrs. Harris leaning close to her.

So that was it. Dyann was going hysterical and Mrs. H. had called for help. Cara smiled and a warm feeling bubbled up inside her. Time for Mighty Mite to take charge.

She twisted the doorknob and went in. Dyann's sobs reverberated in the stuffy air as Cara smiled at Mrs. Harris. "Hi, Mrs. H. What happened?"

"Hello, Cara." Dumpling shaped and white haired, Mrs. Harris was called "Mom" by most of her students. "I'm sorry to get you out of class, but Dyann came into my classroom like this, and she kept asking for you."

Cara approached Dyann. The poor girl was heaving with grief. She held a tight fist to her lips and hugged her bony chest. Tears splashed down her cheeks, and her head lurched every time she sobbed.

"Hey, it's okay," Cara said.

Dyann kept sobbing, and Mrs. Harris handed her a tissue from a box on the desk.

"It's about her editorial on school sports, I suppose?"

"That's it all right."

Cara said to Dyann, "Look, I okayed the story. The principal okayed the story. You are *not* in trouble."

Mrs. Harris said, "She's taken some pretty rough abuse from those athletes."

"It was just an editorial." Dyann's sobs were fraying Cara's nerves. "I don't know what to do with her."

"It's not up to you," Mrs. Harris pointed out. "She has to know that if you express a strong opinion, people will react."

Dyann's whimpering intruded once again. Cara turned to the suffering girl and touched her back. "Dyann, I'll talk to you after school in the library, okay? Just you and me."

Dyann's head lurched again and new sobs convulsed her. Cara said, "I guess she's in no mood to listen now."

"I'm really sorry," Mrs. Harris said.

"No problem." The bell sounded and the hallway outside was filled with sudden noise. Cara picked up her books and said to Dyann, "I'll see you later."

"I'll keep an eye on her," Mrs. Harris said.

"Thanks."

"I'm sorry you had to leave your class."

"It's okay." Cara wasn't sorry. She liked fixing things up. She was thrilled that an editorial in the *Tempest* had caused such a furor. She knew she could straighten out Dyann's head and calm down the jocks. Also, there was a strong chance that she'd win the journalism award this year even though she was only a junior.

Cara tensed her mouth as she shut the bookroom door behind her, but once in the hallway, she let the grin break through.

When lunch period came, Cara got to the cafeteria before the mob and staked out half of a long table. She bought an apple, a package of oatmeal cookies, and a milk, and lined them up neatly in front of her. Then she dragged her notebook and math book out of her canvas tote, fished for a pen in her purse, and arranged her homework next to her lunch. By now, hundreds of kids had poured into the caf, and their roar unnerved her. She was a short girl in a tall universe.

"Cara! How do you get here so fast?"

She looked up and smiled. Nancy Chu tossed her thick hair and smoothed her dark print dress before dropping into a seat.

"I cut outside and through the loading dock."

"Even in the rain?"

"Sure."

Nancy used her purse to pillow her folded arms. "You're so organized."

"I just work things out."

Nancy studied the snaking lunch line. "I'll never get anything. By the time I get in there, it'll be time to go."

"Want one of my cookies?"

Nancy shook her head. "No. I'll try the line." She had a sudden thought. "Hey, I heard Dyann freaked out today."

Cara stopped flipping the pages of her math book. "Who told you that?"

"Everybody knew it."

"I don't see how. Unless Mrs. Harris blabbed."

Nancy laughed. "Now *that's* funny." She pushed away from the table and strode to the food line. Guys on either side of Nancy dribbled chocolate milk as they craned to watch her.

Cara liked being speculated about. She focused on the math problems, blocking out the clamor around her.

"Hey, Caramel."

The pet name made her wince. Then Mark's fingers squeezed her neck and she scrunched up like a turtle. "I *hate* when you do that."

Mark grinned and walked around the table to sit opposite her. "I know."

"I have to finish these problems," she said.

"So finish them."

"Well, don't annoy me."

"Thanks a lot."

She sighed. Why she was so cruel to Mark she didn't know. He was cute and muscular, with a baseball hat worn backward over dirty blond hair, and he was totally in love with her. Having a jock boyfriend should have fulfilled her wildest fantasies—Nancy

Chu didn't even *have* a boyfriend at the moment—but for some bizarre reason, Cara tormented the poor dolt.

"You're not annoying me," she said. "It's been a crazy day."

"Yeah, tell me about it."

"Okay," she said. "See, it all started when . . ."

Mark stared blankly at her. She shook her head. "It was humor," she explained. "See, I said I had a crazy day and you said tell me about it so I was telling you about it."

"Yeah?"

"Telling you about it. Like you didn't *really* want me to tell you about it but I was telling you about it. Okay, delete, forget it."

"Wrong time of the month?"

Cara shot him a death look. "You are such a jerk."

He brooded while she viciously scribbled equations. Then he broke the silence.

"So what did you say to Dyann?"

Cara flipped her pencil aside. "Was this event on CNN or something?"

"Just asking."

"I didn't say much. She was crying the whole time."

"Yeah?" Mark leaned forward.

Cara said, "You're disgusting. You *did* this to her."

"We didn't write the article."

"Editorial."

"Whatever."

"And you misunderstood everything she said. She wasn't attacking the sports program at Westfield. She

5

was just saying that the arts should get equal funding."

"She called us smelly animals."

Cara smirked. Dyann *had* called them smelly animals, and other things too. "She was using colorful language."

"Colorful lies."

"Calm down, Mark. It's all being blown out of proportion."

"Yeah, well, I can see whose side you're on."

"I'm not taking sides. I'm the editor."

"You're her friend."

"Not really."

Mark draped his arms on the back of his chair. "We're going to demand that Dyann get kicked off the paper."

"Give it up."

"We're getting signatures on a petition."

"You can petition all you want. It's not going to happen."

Mark tipped his chair back. "We'll go over your head, to Mr. Brill."

"He okayed the editorial. I have the typed copy with his initials on it."

"He can change his mind."

"No way."

Mark let his chair fall back down with a crash. "You're not unbeatable, Cara. You're not Supergirl."

"Yeah, uh-huh." She stared hard at her notebook.

His hand clamped over her wrist and her head snapped up. He said, "Don't ignore me!"

"Are you *nuts?*" she whispered.

6

He took his hand away and reddened. "Sorry."

"Smelly animals is right!"

Nancy returned with a tray of food. "Hi, Mark," she said as she put down the tray and sat. "Should I sit somewhere else?"

"Why?" he said.

Nancy eagerly unwrapped her meatball hero. "I don't know. In case you wanted to talk love talk."

Mark made a vulgar noise, and Cara said, "Don't worry about it."

"Oops, sorry." Nancy's cheeks flushed and she stared intently at her food. "I was going to ask about your sweet sixteen party, but maybe it's a bad time."

"No," Cara said. "You can ask."

"Well, where is it?" Nancy asked, biting into her sandwich. "Who's coming? Tell me everything."

"It's at the Swan Club, and I haven't finished the list yet," Cara said. "I have to talk to my mom and dad about numbers."

Mark looked at each of them. 'Isn't this supposed to be a surprise?"

"I didn't want a surprise party," Cara said. "I hate them. Everybody looks dumb yelling surprise and I don't have the fun of planning the party."

Mark laughed. "Yeah, I guess you'd want to plan the whole thing. Everything perfect."

"That's right," Cara said, biting the words. "Everything perfect."

"Don't listen to him," Nancy urged. "Guys don't understand."

"Damn straight," Mark pouted. He stood up, slammed his chair against the table, and stalked

7

away, earning some stares. Cara felt her neck get warm.

"What happened?" Nancy asked.

"PMS."

"Huh?"

"Permanent Male Stupidity."

Nancy giggled. Slurping chocolate milk, she said, "You guys are the original odd couple."

"I guess so." It annoyed her that she disliked Mark and stayed with him. Why? To show she could manage a romance just like she managed the newspaper? She was sorry now that she'd been rotten to him. She imagined dancing with him at her sweet sixteen, with the lights spinning.

Nancy asked, "What are you grinning about?"

"Lust."

"Oh, okay." Nancy took another bite of her hero and then erupted into laughter.

That night Cara had planned to sit cross-legged on her jade carpet, working on her invitation list. Instead, she navigated the icy path to Dyann's town house, with a March wind freezing her face off. Luckily, her mom had a meeting so she was taking the car out anyway and didn't mind dropping Cara off. "I'll pick you up when I'm done," she told her.

"You can pick me up in ten minutes," Cara said.

"Be calm," Mom said. "This comes with being editor-in-chief."

No, it came with knowing Dyann Wilson. After school, Cara had gone to the library and waited, but Dyann never showed up. Finally Cara went to the main office and had the secretary page Dyann. No luck.

So Cara asked to use the phone on the receptionist's desk and called Dyann. Dyann answered. "You're *home?*" Cara cried.

"Yes. I got a pounding headache and I went home early."

"I've just waited an hour for you! You could have left a message!"

"Sorry."

Cara glared at the empty corridor. "Do you want me to come over and talk?"

"If you like."

"Dyann, I've got to make *plans!* Do you need to talk?"

"If you have plans, go ahead," Dyann said.

"I think we need to talk," Cara said coldly. "How about if I come over tonight about seven?"

"Okay."

"You'll be home, right?"

"I suppose."

Cara slammed down the phone and quietly raged in the empty office. Dyann was an incredible writer, but she alienated everyone with her attitude.

So now, at seven-fifteen on a bitter night, Cara stood shivering in Dyann's living room, her hands in her coat pockets. Dyann shut the door.

"Pretty cold out?" Dyann asked.

Cara glared at her. "Yeah, it's pretty cold." Dyann looked like one of those special effects ghosts in movies: kind of beautiful but transparent. She wore a T-shirt nightdress over her willowy body and her long, straight hair spilled over her shoulders. She gazed at Cara from big, moist eyes.

Cara dropped her coat on a railing by the door. Glancing up the stairs, she asked, "Is your mom home?"

"No. You want something?"

"Rum."

"I don't know if we've got any."

"I wasn't serious."

Cara dropped into a big upholstered chair in front of a new big-screen TV. Dyann's mom worked for the town, but she got alimony from Dyann's dad so she could afford this neat place. With Cara's dad in and out of work, *they* sure couldn't buy a fancy TV.

Dyann nested on an ottoman. "Well, go ahead. Give me therapy."

"Don't be a hag, Dyann. You were totally stressed out before. We thought you were going to seizure."

Hair curtained Dyann's face, and she seemed to stare at nothing. "I'm sorry I overreacted."

"So talk about it."

"Talk about what? I exposed this school district as a cultural wasteland."

"I know what the editorial said," Cara told her. "That's not the problem."

"It is the problem," Dyann retorted. "I am being verbally assaulted by the athletes in this school, and their coach is allowing them to do it."

"Coach Franklin isn't like that."

"I forgot. Your boyfriend is one of them."

"Dyann, they're just pissed off."

"About what? The truth?"

Something about Dyann's tone of voice made Cara

want to drive a truck over her. "They think you're attacking the sports program."

Dyann smiled bitterly and pushed her hair over one shoulder. "Is that what you think too? You said the column was good."

"It is good. You write better than anybody."

"So defend it."

"I *did* defend it. What do you think I've been doing?"

"I don't know." Dyann brushed an angry hand across her eyes. "In economics, Joey Bianco and Carl Ward sit behind me and whisper filth into my ear the whole period. I told Mr. Ackerman that I was being harassed and he said to change my seat. What about changing Joey Bianco's seat? But Ackerman's afraid of them. Everyone's afraid of them."

"I'm really sorry, Dyann. I didn't know all this was happening."

"Well, nobody's doing it to *you*."

"That's dumb!" Cara snapped. "I told Mark he was being a moron. I'll talk to Mr. Brill tomorrow."

"Oh, our esteemed faculty adviser. He's a jock himself."

"You're being unfair," Cara responded. "Mr. Brill has done a lot to make the *Tempest* better. He got us the Medalist award from Columbia."

Dyann leaned against the banister. "I didn't think you'd badmouth him. He made you editor in your junior year."

"I *worked* for that."

"I guess kissing up is work."

Cara stormed out of her chair and stood with her fists tightly clenched. "Get off it, Dyann. I don't have to be dumped on. I take responsibility for what's published in the *Tempest*.''

Dyann stared at the wall. ''Nobody's going to take my side. I should have seen it, but you do a good job of getting people hyped up. Now I have to be crucified.''

''That's really paranoid, Dyann.''

''It's true.''

''Forget this,'' Cara said. ''I have homework to do.''

She ran over and grabbed her coat from the railing. Dyann followed her with her eyes. ''Where are you going? You said your mom's not picking you up till nine.''

Cara swore.

Dyann grabbed the remote from the coffee table and switched on the set. ''So let's watch TV and have some chips.''

Cara stared at her. ''You're whacked, Dyann.''

Dyann curled up on the ottoman, her chin tucked on her knees. ''Why?''

''We just had a major brawl. Now you want to act like this is a sleep-over?''

Dyann tapped the remote against her chin and gazed at the screen. ''We're still friends, right?''

''Before or after I make a voodoo doll?''

''Don't joke about it!''

Cara shook her head and reluctantly dropped to the carpet. ''Okay, don't have a fit.'' She felt tired and miserable. She'd wasted her evening and Dyann had dished her over.

Dyann said, ''I didn't mean to bite your head off. How about if I make some dip?''

Some of Cara's fury melted. "Okay. Sure."

What a sap she was. Two nice words from Dyann were enough to make Cara believe she could still control the situation. And she *could*. After she lived through the next two hours of Dyann's philosophy and MTV.

CHAPTER

2

Bless the window, Dyann thought. To be exact, the second window from the front of the room. That was Dyann's escape window. While Mrs. Oslansky whined about note cards, Dyann cupped her chin on her palm and gazed outside.

The window looked out on an expanse of lawn, pale and hard from winter. Directly across she could study the cream-colored brick of the school's entrance. Today there was bright, harsh sun and intense blue sky. Kids hurried along the sidewalk. Dyann regretted opening up to Cara. She kept her soul locked away from the others. None of them could give her anything; none of them tried.

Mrs. Oslansky whined, "The note cards may be typed or handwritten, but they must be on four-by-six cards. Each card must have a slug—"

Dyann smiled at the image of slugs on the note cards. A finger poked her back. She stiffened, and the voice behind her whispered, "Can you change a flat?"

She'd forgotten that Mark Lanier sat behind her. Grimly, she kept her eyes on the window.

"You better learn."

She swallowed back tears. Every day he did this. She hadn't told Cara that Mark was part of it. Only that Joey and Carl were.

"Well, you're pretty flat, so maybe you do know."

"Shut up!" she whispered fiercely.

Mrs. Oslansky looked at her. Dyann's face grew hot.

I wish I could hurt them, Dyann thought. She imagined nailing Mark's hands to the desk. She imagined each finger snapping as he shrieked in unspeakable pain.

"Every note you take should be on a different card," Mrs. Oslansky whined. "Otherwise, you won't be able to put them in order."

Mrs. Oslansky sat primly on her desk. She spoke always in the same tone, at the same pitch. Forty minutes of torture, relieved only by the window.

Mark poked her again. "Four flats," he whispered. *"P-s-s-s-h-h-h-h-h."*

Stop it, she pleaded.

Mrs. Oslansky said, "Is there a problem?"

Dyann bit down hard on her lip and shook her head.

"Then stop making bizarre noises."

She heard the jocks laugh again. Why didn't Mrs. Oslansky hear it? She probably did, but wouldn't take on those guys. Dyann doodled with her pen as she sought refuge in the window.

Yet the window could hurt too. The brilliant sky made her see Washington Square Park in New York City and the red walls of NYU. She saw herself bundled in scarf and wool cap, talking with Myra and her other friends. Exciting friends, who took her to outrageous parties, where she danced with thousands of beautiful people, in parking lots or under the Queensboro Bridge. Only then did she feel alive and free.

Mark poked her again, but she forced herself not to move. Mrs. Oslansky didn't notice. "You have four weeks to do the paper, so the note cards should be finished by next Tuesday. . . ."

Who cares? she screamed silently. Why hadn't anyone asked whether she wanted to stay with her father? He was a computer artist, not a psychopath. There wasn't any work for him on Long Island, where *Mother* had wanted to live. It made perfect sense for him to move back to the city after the separation, and perfect sense for Dyann to move there too.

Her mother had convinced the family court judge it wouldn't be healthy. Drug dealers and homeless scum infested the city. Dad sometimes forgot to come home when he found a "companion" he liked. Sometimes there was only a bottle of Bailey's in the refrigerator. *I don't care,* Dyann had cried. *My friends take care of me.*

"I'll personally check over ten sample note cards and write comments for you. . . ."

Nobody listened. Dyann was dragged back to Westfield, where everybody spent Saturday night drinking and puking.

Mark belched behind her. Everyone cracked up. Mrs. Oslansky glared, but at least she couldn't blame Dyann. Mrs. Oslansky waited for the laughter to subside and went on.

Dyann swore she'd get back to New York City, even if she had to run away. Her mom didn't know about the Long Island Rail Road schedules hidden in her bureau drawer. The cops would go to her father's apartment and he'd say she wasn't there.

The classroom door opened. It was Eddie Belmonte. Derisive laughter rippled through the room, and Mrs. Oslansky looked pained.

Eddie shuffled up to her and held out a crumpled piece of paper. Dyann found Eddie sad, not funny. His baseball cap, dark sunglasses, and long khaki trench coat had to be hiding a lot of pain. He wasn't stupid, she knew that. He hardly ever said anything, always coming late to class with a pass from some teacher or other. He usually sat in the back, studying a map of New York State and circling towns with a red pen.

Eddie ambled down the aisle, his unlaced boots clunking on the tile floor. He glanced at Dyann as he passed and raised a finger in greeting. She nodded back. He slid into his seat and stared wherever he was staring behind those shades, a half smile on his face.

Dyann faced front again. Eddie always acknowledged her, even though he never spoke to her. She was the only one he interacted with. She smiled to herself. Maybe she'd take him back to the city with her. He'd like it there. He was probably dying in Westfield as she was.

Maybe they'd kill Mark together. And Cara. Make it look like a double suicide. Then go to the city and never be humiliated again.

Mark belched. Mrs. Oslansky kept whining, white hands folded in the lap of her dark skirt. Dyann looked out the window, reaching for the glittering sunlight, pretending it was city sunlight, pretending she was in her dad's apartment, pretending she could go outside and be free.

Help me, she pleaded. She concentrated on the thought, trying to send it to Eddie. She didn't think he was receiving anything, even though she could feel his eyes on the back of her neck.

That afternoon Cara, Nancy, and Dyann started working on the April issue of the *Tempest.* Also with them were Thea Greco, a petite wisp of a girl, and Nick Berge, a senior who'd lost out to Cara for the editor-in-chief job.

"Okay, stories for April," Cara said. The school newspaper office was partitioned from a classroom by a modular wall. Cara was perched on a long shelf that held two MAC LC computers and a LASERWRITER, along with schoolbooks and coats.

"Senior class trip," Nancy volunteered.

"Naturally," Cara said. Nancy jotted it down in a small spiral notebook.

"School budget," Nick said. He leaned against a wall of cabinets.

"We'll have to get that information from the district office," Cara said. "Nancy, make a note to call them."

"Okay, chief."

"And don't call me chief."

Everyone laughed. Cara smiled and said, "Teacher profile of the month, student profile of the month, what else?"

Nick said, "How about Dyann does a follow-up on her jock expose: Do Your Tax Dollars Support Towel-Snapping Tournaments?"

Nancy's eyes narrowed. "That was incredibly stupid."

"But funny."

Cara said, "You really have to keep the warped humor under control, Nick."

"Not your call."

"It is *so* my call."

Dyann made a time-out sign. "Okay, okay. No bodily contact."

"Let's get back to the newspaper," Cara said. "What else goes in for April?"

Nancy said, "Usual stuff, no? Editorial, letters, sports, reviews . . ."

"Music and culture column," Dyann offered.

Cara looked at her. "What kind of music and culture?"

"Classical music. Art museums. Dance. Theater. It's all around Long Island. People should know about it."

"People will go into a coma," Nick said.

"At least they'll read it."

Cara liked the bickering, now that she wasn't the target. "Okay, Dyann. You have at least one reader, so let's try the column."

"Thanks."

Nick said, "Just don't mention jocks."

Dyann smiled and looked at the floor. Cara said, "Anything else? We have space."

Thea raised her hand.

"Yes, Thea?"

"Horoscope column."

Nancy said, "Hey, yeah!"

Nick snorted. Cara said, "Oh, not that."

"Why not?" Dyann asked.

"It's junior high stuff," Nick said. "You will find love lurking around the corner today. Beware a stranger wearing feathers."

Cara said, "It's too tabloid."

"You don't believe in it?" Dyann asked.

"No. Do you?"

"Yes."

"No way! You're too educated."

Dyann smiled. "Educated people accept the paranormal."

"Come on. You believe that the position of a ball of hot gas seven billion miles away affects your life?"

"It's possible."

Nancy said, "I'm a Gemini and what they say about us is *exactly* like me!"

"Nancy, you're *making* it fit you. And even if it does, there must be a billion Geminis out there. You think they all have the same personality?"

Dyann said, "Psychic readings are personal and intimate."

Nick sang the "Twilight Zone" theme. Cara said, "But Thea's not a psychic."

"My aunt is," Thea said.

Nancy gaped at her. "Cool!"

Dyann stared intently at Thea. "Does she live around here?"

"Northport."

Cara said. "Thea, you really know about all this stuff?"

Thea shrugged. "No, I just thought it would be fun to have an astrology column."

Cara knew she was being spiteful, but the words came anyway. "I'm sorry, Thea. I'm sure you'd do a good job, but it just doesn't feel right. Okay?"

"Sure."

Nancy said, "Aw, Cara. It'd be neat."

"But I said no, Nancy."

"Okay, okay, don't freak." She vigorously crossed out words she had written in the notebook.

Nick said, "Careful, Cara, Thea will put a spell on you."

"Shut up!" Dyann snapped.

Cara didn't like admitting that she'd killed a good idea just because Dyann liked it. "Well," she said. "We still need more news."

Thea gasped.

"What's wrong?" Cara asked.

Nick said, "We have company."

She followed his thumb and saw a tall guy in a cap and army trench coat, standing motionless in the doorway of the room. Sunglasses hid his eyes but Cara knew he was staring at her.

"Eddie Belmonte," she said quietly.

"Who's Eddie Belmonte?" Thea wanted to know.

Nancy said, "A total weirdo. Everyone says he's into black magic."

Cara tried to look at him without being obvious. Her heart raced. "What is that creep doing here?"

Dyann shrugged. "Ask him."

"No way. Nick?"

Nick acted pained. "I figured I'd get the job." He reluctantly stood up.

Thea said, "Maybe he wants to join the newspaper."

Nick said, "Yeah, and write *dispatches from hell*."

Nancy giggled. Cara said, "Go ask him!"

"Cover me," Nick said. He slowly moved toward the door of the partition, then abruptly stopped. "He's gone."

"He couldn't be!" Cara said. She looked, but saw nobody standing in the doorway now. "Check the hallway," Cara said.

Nick said, "If he's not here, I'm not looking for him."

Dyann said, "I don't think he's dangerous."

"How do *you* know?" Thea asked.

Nick said, "He's probably her lover."

"Gross." Nancy made a face.

"Enough," Cara said. "He probably was looking for someone and realized he was at the wrong room."

Nancy grinned. "Logical as always, Mr. Spock."

"Well, someone has to be." She sighed. *"Anyway,* let's get a paper together. Nick, you figure out the sports stuff and we'll do the reviews and features. Time is tight, so let's get cracking."

"Sieg, heil!" Nick cried.

"Not funny," Cara said.

Nancy stood up. "Are you sticking around, Cara?"

"No. I'm meeting my mom to go shopping."

Cara gathered her books and said goodbye to everyone. At the door she touched Thea's shoulder and said, "Don't hate me. I have to make these decisions."

Thea gave her a smile. "It's okay."

Cara squeezed her arm and walked into the deserted corridor. Angry at herself, she took the stairs two at a time.

CHAPTER

3

On Saturday Cara went with her mom and dad to the Swan Club to make arrangements for her sweet sixteen party. Cara stood in the parking lot, studying the white and gray building. "It's kind of small," she said.

Mom stood next to her while Dad locked the car. "Well, we're only having fifty people. Catering halls won't book an affair for that few."

She quickly linked her hands around her mom's wrist. "It's okay."

Mom smiled a brave smile. All of her mom's smiles were brave ones. Getting up at four in the morning every day to work in the Westfield High School cafeteria was pretty tough.

Looking behind her, Cara watched her dad limp around a puddle. "Come on, slowpoke," she shouted. "You'd better dance faster than that."

"Yeah," he said. "I'll dance fast. I'll dance *half-fast!*"

Cara groaned at the bad joke. She could almost feel the pain in Dad's bad leg, but he never mentioned it. Dad was a big man, which didn't help; he had to work at moving his bulk around.

When he reached them, Cara went to him and hugged him. "You're slow, but you're still handsome."

He ruffled her hair. "I'm already payin' as much as I'm gonna pay."

She hugged him more tightly, then took his hand and led him toward the building. When she was a little girl, he'd pick her up and she'd wrap her arms and legs around him while he let go. They called it an octopus hug. She wasn't much taller now than she had been then, but her weight had been redistributed so there were no more octopus hugs.

Cara examined the room while Mom and Dad went to find the party manager. The Swan Club was mostly a hangout for the over twenty-one crowd. It had a stone fireplace near the dance floor, and the deejay's light scaffold stood black and menacing. Looking up, Cara could see skylights one floor above.

Mom and Dad returned with a tired-looking man of about fifty. He wore a stained white shirt and a dorky blue tie. "Cara," Mom said, "this is Mr. Terranova."

"Hi, Cara," Mr. Terranova said with a phony smile.

"Hi." *Mr. New Earth,* Cara translated, remembering her two years of Italian. "Do we get the whole place?"

"Sure," Mr. Terranova said. "Everything you see."

"Okay." Cara indicated the staircase leading to the second floor. "What's up there?"

"Couches, tables. People like to go up there to take a rest."

"Nobody's resting at my party," she said. "I don't see the deejay's rig, just his lights."

"Oh, that's upstairs."

"Upstairs? How's he going to know what's going on down here?"

Mr. Terranova glanced oddly at Mom and Dad. "It works fine, you'll see."

"I don't know. I think the deejay should be down here."

Mr. Terranova said, sotto voce, to Mom and Dad, "Maybe we can talk in my office."

Dad eyed his daughter. "This is her party. She calls the shots."

The words warmed her. She remembered him before his injury. He was a floor tiler. Once or twice Cara had gone with him to watch him eyeball a corner of a room, then unerringly cut an odd piece of tile with his magical cutting machine. She always got a thrill when he fit the fragment in like the last piece of a jigsaw puzzle.

Then he was hit by a car coming out of a 7-Eleven. It was a banged-up Monte Carlo. The police guessed it was a kid, wasted and cutting across the parking lot to avoid a traffic light. Nobody ever found the car, or the driver.

"Cara, are you listening?" Mom's voice asked.

"Uh, sure. What was the question?"

Mom laughed. "The food. Ziti or stuffed shells?"

"Both."

Mom's eyes narrowed, not a good sign. "Come on, baby. I still have to pick up socks for Brian."

"Mom, Brian is twenty-two years old. Why can't he go to a store and pick out socks?"

"He's out in Oregon."

"They wear socks in Oregon!"

Dad grunted. "She'll buy socks for him when he's fifty."

"Why not?" Mom asked. "I still buy 'em for you."

Cara felt a strong wash of love for her parents. Sometimes they were pretty thickheaded, but they got Andrea into med school and Brian into physical therapy school, and Cara knew that they'd sell their souls to get her into business school.

"How come we can't have ziti and stuffed shells?" she asked.

Mr. Terranova said, "Well, you can have anything you want if you pay for it. The package your folks are looking at gives you chicken parmigiana with a choice of ziti or shells."

"And how much is that a person?"

Alarmed, Mr. Terranova turned to her Dad. Dad shrugged. "Tell her."

"Twenty-five a person."

"Fifty bucks a couple for *that?*" Cara said.

Mr. Terranova twined his hands in front of him, as if praying. "It's a good deal, missy. Includes salad and the cake and hors d'oeuvres—"

"What kind of hors d'oeuvres?"

He shook his head and said, "Pigs in blankets, little knishes, little pizza rolls—"

"Oh, like the stuff Mom buys in the Price Club."

27

She would have liked the Crestwood Country Club, where Jessica Candalorio had *her* sweet sixteen, but she knew her mom and dad couldn't afford it. Mom and Dad had always taught her not to whine or throw tantrums, just to dust herself off and get to work.

She sat at one of the empty tables and stared at her parents. "Do you think it's a fair price?"

Dad spread his hands. "Up to you."

Cara's heart beat faster as she decided on her next move. "I don't think it's a great deal. The place is small and the deejay is upstairs and the price is like out of sight."

Mr. Terranova looked like he was going to spit marbles. "You won't get a better deal, not in April. You're talking the height of the wedding season."

"Who's going to get married here?" Cara said. "Munchkins?"

Mom said, "Cara!"

"Sorry. Anyway, let's look somewhere else."

She stood up, smoothing her school jacket impudently. She caught her dad's eye, and he leveled a gaze at her that said, *This better work or you're having your party in the backyard.*

Mr. Terranova stared at Mom and Dad in disbelief. "You're not going to talk this over?"

"Like I told you," Dad said, "it's her party."

Cara forced her legs not to tremble as she brushed past Mr. Terranova and gestured for her mom and dad to come with her. Mom stood up and slipped her purse over her shoulder.

"Jeez," Mr. Terranova said. "Listen, if I give you shells and ziti would you find it acceptable?"

Cara grinned, still facing the door. Altering her expression, she turned and eyed the place again. "It's still kind of high."

Mr. Terranova locked eyes with her. "I can't come down any more in the price, missy. Not with what I'm giving you."

Cara glanced at Dad, who raised his eyebrows. She said. "Okay, I guess, but I still want to talk about the deejay being downstairs."

Mr. Terranova waved a hand in resignation. "Like I said, it's whatever you want, but I don't recommend it."

Cara couldn't resist a smile. She impulsively went to Dad and hugged him, then Mom.

Mr. Terranova said, "Come on, I'll write out the contract." He looked at Cara with one cocked eye. "Do you let your parents come in while we sign it?"

Cara laughed. Suddenly she couldn't wait for the party.

Rain streaked the window of Dyann's room as she lay stomach down on her bed and tapped out Myra's phone number. As she pressed the receiver hard against her ear, she gazed at the framed art gallery prints on her black wall. *She'd* painted her room black, and put in the ultraviolet lights. Her mother wanted her to get counseling for that too.

"Yes?"

"Hi, Myra. It's Dyann."

"Oh, Dyann. How are you?"

"I'm suicidal. I miss you guys so much."

"Life pretty dull in the 'burbs?"

"Boredom is the leading cause of death out here. How's it going in the Apple? Any jobs?"

"Some runway stuff. No TV series yet."

Dyann smiled. They always joked about how Myra would become a TV star. "Any day now," she said.

"Yeah, any day. So what made you call?"

"Like you didn't know!"

"Didn't know what?"

She rolled onto her back and twined the phone wire around her wrist. "I read about it in the paper, Myra. How you and Paul are going to be out on the Island next week to do a revue for the Caldwell Playhouse."

Myra laughed. "Oh, right. Punishment for our sins."

"More like a miracle as far as I'm concerned."

"Well, I don't know about that. But Ted Balaban asked us and we couldn't say no. Besides, he's paying actual money and we need some."

"I know, I know. Anyway, how about I drop by to applaud like crazy and we can hit the clubs out here? They're not the city but pretty decent."

Silence greeted Dyann. Then Myra said, "Well, it's going to be tough, hon. We're doing eight shows a week, and I already have a bunch of parties to hit. I'll be lucky if I don't get shipped home in a box."

Dyann had pinned all her hopes on Myra. She saw herself driving back to New York City with them, her duffel bag in the trunk. She saw herself crashing with Myra, finding a job. She'd made herself believe Myra was her lifeline.

"Come on," she said. "Not one night? Afternoon? Anything? I really miss you guys."

"Hon, I'm sorry. But see the show anyway. Bring some school chums and hit the clubs with them."

She felt herself sucked through the window, into

the rain. "I don't have any school chums, Myra. You're my chums. You're all I have."

Myra said, "Eek. That's a heavy guilt trip."

Dyann watched the ceiling blur. "I'm sorry. I thought we were friends."

"Dyann, honey, it was great adopting you last summer, but you can't live with us."

Bang bang bang went the nails into the coffin. Inside the coffin Dyann clawed and screamed. "Okay. I get the message."

"Hey, sweetie, we never gave you any other message."

"Have a good show, Myra. I probably won't get there."

Myra sighed. "Kid, you always were pretty weird. Take care of yourself."

"Thanks. You're too kind." She heard Myra click off, but held the phone for a long moment. The sobs came on like tidal surges. She couldn't take this blow, not this one.

"God, no," she choked. Her body couldn't hold this much defeat.

Vaguely, through her grief, she heard the doorbell ringing downstairs. Mother was out, so Dyann had to answer. She sat up, her head thudding. The doorbell rang again.

She hung up the phone and walked down the stairs. "Who is it?"

"Eddie."

The name didn't mean anything. She unlocked the door and opened it.

Eddie. From school. He looked insanely wrong there, the baseball hat pulled down, the trench coat collar pulled up. And he wore sunglasses, even at night.

Dyann felt ice between her shoulders. "What do you want?"

"I have an idea for the paper."

"*What?*"

"About the astrology column."

It took a minute for her to make sense of this. Then she remembered that Eddie had stood in the doorway during the *Tempest* meeting. "You came to my house to talk about the *newspaper?*"

"Take Cara to Aunt June."

"Look, Eddie, I'm really beat right now and I don't know what the hell you're talking about." Cold air had rushed in around Eddie and swept the breath from her lungs.

"Thea's aunt, the psychic—take Cara to her."

"How did you know her name was June?"

"I checked."

Shivering, Dyann said, "Why would Cara go there?"

"Tell her it'd make a good story."

"Eddie, what's the point?"

"Get back at her."

Dyann stared at him. "Get back at her for what?"

"You know."

Yes, she knew, but how did he know? "I don't think it would do much good."

"You'd have power over her. She'd lose control."

"Why are you so interested in getting Cara?"

He smiled. "I'm interested in you."

Quivering from the cold, she said, "Eddie, you're a strange guy and I'm not in the mood."

"Give it some thought."

"Okay, I will. I'll think about it."

He looked forlorn, like he'd really expected to be asked in. But he just flashed another quick smile and walked away. She shut the door, shuddering, then rushed back up to her room.

The house ticked more loudly. Dyann's brain was alive with vengeful scenarios. She'd have to enlist Cara's friend Nancy in this, so Cara would agree to it. And Nick, and Thea.

She shut her swollen eyes. Cara would just laugh.

But if she didn't? And as Eddie said, it would take away some of Cara's control.

Dyann's mind buzzed like a nest of killer bees. She hugged her pillow and had a fantasy of Eddie slicing Cara's throat with razored gloves.

CHAPTER

4

*W*hy? Cara thought as she stared out the side window of Nancy's Honda. Rain shivered on the glass as they drove past shuttered storefronts. Telephone wires swung like jump ropes in the wind. *All we need is thunder and lightning.*

"Are you awake?" Nancy asked.

Cara snapped out of her trance. "I'm just wondering why I agreed to this."

"It'll be neat," Nancy said. She looked adorable in her Westfield kickline jacket. Behind Cara, Nick, Dyann, and Thea sat quietly. *Too quietly,* Cara thought.

"Yeah, neat," she said. "For seventy-five bucks, it'd better be outrageous."

Nancy suggested, "Why don't we bill it to the *Tempest?*"

Cara laughed. "Yeah, right. I can see giving Mr. Brill an invoice for a psychic reading."

A gust of wind rocked the car. Cara hoped her mom didn't find out about this. It was bad enough she had lied about going to a movie, but seventy-five dollars for a fortune-teller—well, even her mom probably wouldn't believe that.

Dyann asked, "Are you nervous?"

Cara leaned back against the seat. "No, I'm not nervous. I'm pissed off about wasting my time and my money."

"You shouldn't go," Thea said. "Aunt June will know you're hostile."

"She'd *better* know I'm hostile," Cara said. "She'd better know a lot more than that."

"Don't test her," Thea said. "You'll waste the whole visit."

Cara felt anger tighten her throat. "The visit is already a waste."

Nancy said, "Come on, it's investigative reporting."

"It's dumb."

"So let's turn around," Nancy snapped. "I can be home watching soap operas."

Cara stared at Nancy. "Well, excuse *me*. I didn't know you were so hot for this."

Nancy sighed. "I'm sorry. But it's like sometimes you're so unbending, you know? Lighten up a little."

"Okay, I'm light. I'm practically weightless."

The whole car got quiet. Cara knew a lot of her anger was self-directed. She needed to pit herself against this stupid psychic and Dyann. How Dyann had gotten control of this situation, Cara didn't know. She'd been working in the bookroom, stamping books for Mrs. Harris, when Dyann and Thea and Nick had barged in. After about twelve seconds of small talk, Dyann had said, "A lot of kids in this school go to psychics."

Cara looked up and said, "Why are you telling me this?"

Nick said, "You put this stuff down at the meeting."

"Yeah, so?"

"Well, a lot of kids are into it. It's a trend."

Cara put down her stamp and sat back. "Okay, what's up?"

Dyann leaned against a metal bookshelf. "Wouldn't this kind of fad make a good story for the paper?"

"Are we back with the horoscope column?"

"No," Dyann said. "Something a lot better."

Cara focused on Thea, who hung back in the doorway. "Was this your idea?"

Thea lowered her eyes. "No."

Nick blurted, "We think it would be great if you went to Thea's aunt and then wrote about it."

Cara knew that was it. "If you think that would be great, why don't *you* go? Or Dyann? Or just let Thea write about her aunt."

Dyann flipped her hair aside. "The whole idea would be for a doubter to do it. That would make the story."

"Unless you're nervous about it," Nick added.

Cara made a face. "Nick, you are so obvious it's grotesque. Is there a bet going?"

"No," Dyann said. "It just seemed like a good idea. But you're the editor."

"You're worse than Nick," Cara said. The coldness had spread to her limbs now, numbing her hands. She really didn't want to do this; she also knew that she *had* to go.

"Okay, look," she said. "I'll do it if you'll promise to shut up about it afterward and let me get on with my life."

"Great," Dyann said.

Nick made a fist and chanted, "Go, Cara; go, Cara—"

"Help!" Cara sighed.

That's how it happened. A stupid dare and Cara had taken the bait. Nancy was driving down a local road now. "Okay, Thea, where do I turn?"

"Second left."

Cara heard Thea whisper something to Dyann, but she couldn't make out the words. Nancy put on her turn signal and nearly cut off an oncoming car. Nick said, "We're almost there, Cara. Are you *ready?*"

"Grow up," Cara said. "Maybe she'll tell me when you'll die."

Thea said, "A reading is always positive."

Cara laughed. "Only good news."

Dyann said, "A psychic will only give you a bad prediction if you can do something about it."

"Left here," Thea said.

Nancy swung the steering wheel. They drove between stone gates into an apartment complex. Cara said, "She won't tell me when I'm going to die?"

"Not if it can't be prevented."

"Well, I'll sure *try* to prevent it." She fought the knotted feeling in her chest. "What is this place?"

"Crestwood Gardens," Thea said.

"She's in an apartment?"

Nick said, "Where did you think she'd be? In a crumbling old mansion with a *strange light in the window?*"

Nancy said, "Will you guys cut it out? I'm trying to see a number!"

Nick pressed his fingertips to his head and shut his eyes. "Is the number—*forty-seven?*"

"Jerk!" Cara said.

Thea said, "Park here."

Nancy eased into a parking space and stopped the car. With the motor off, they were swept into sudden silence. Rain clattered on the car. The red bricks of the apartment buildings were dark and wet.

"Go ahead," Nancy said. "We'll wait in the car."

"You owe me for this," Cara told them as she unbuckled.

It's a setup, Cara reassured herself. She sat in a puffy leather chair opposite June, who had turned part of the living room of her apartment into a kind of office. Vertical blinds blocked the window and light came from two lamps. Cara's eyes roamed over white lacquered bookshelves.

"I'm going to tape the session," June said. She indicated a portable cassette recorder on the lamp table next to her chair. "You can have the tape afterward."

"Why?"

June smiled. "So you can refer to it again. It's hard to remember everything."

Cara couldn't help thinking, *Aren't you worried that I'll use it against you?* Thea's aunt June turned out to be a tall, tailored woman in a coffee-colored blouse and a tweed skirt. She wore her hair in a short cut and her face was friendly but stern.

"I guess it's okay," Cara said.

June studied Cara for a moment. "You're here to get a story for your school paper?"

"Thea told you that!"

"Yes, of course she did."

Cara breathed out hard. "Sorry."

June sat up a little straighter. "Do you want a reading or just an interview?"

"Huh?"

"Well, if you'd like to ask me questions about psychic readings, I'll answer them. If you want me to *do* a reading for you, that's something different."

Cara's stomach lurched. "I didn't know I had a choice."

"You always have a choice," June said. "You're a young lady who likes to make choices, who likes to be in control."

"Did Thea tell you that too?"

"No." June leaned forward. "I'm also a psychologist."

"You are?" Cara wished she didn't sound so dumb.

"Yes. My psi abilities help me in doing therapy, but I don't give psychic readings to patients. I keep that for here."

"That's really interesting," Cara said. "I didn't think a psychic could be a psychologist."

"Same prefix, right?"

"I guess so."

June's eyes were gray and gentle. "I think you

want me to give you a reading, but you're afraid of what might happen.''

"More psychology?"

"Yes. If you put me on trial, you'll block out what I need to know. Would you like some time to decide?"

She had already decided. Maybe it was June's niceness, or her own anger at Dyann, but no way was she going to chicken out. "I'd like a reading," she said. Her voice cracked a little.

"Okay." June sat back. "I'd like you to do a little deep breathing, Cara. You need to untense a little."

"Are you going to hypnotize me?"

A brief smile. "No. Just relax you."

Heart pounding, Cara leaned back hard and gripped the arms of the chair. She felt just as she did in the dentist's office just before he drilled. Shutting her eyes, she sucked in a deep, rattling breath and forced it out.

"Calm down," June said. "You'll hyperventilate."

Cara blushed. "Sorry."

"Don't be so tough on yourself. You're not competing with anyone."

Cara opened her eyes and forced herself to breathe more slowly.

"That's better," June said. "I begin to see you now. There was so much anxiety, it was like a wall." She looked at Cara, her eyes half-closed. "You like to be needed, to solve things. Some of it is compensating for your size, but you don't obsess over being petite. I hear a phrase—'Mighty Mite.' Does someone call you that?"

Cara's temples throbbed. "I call myself that." *Stay loose, Cara. They told her all this.*

"And 'Caramel.' Who calls you that?"

"My boyfriend."

June's face puckered a little. "I don't see a romantic relationship. I see another boy, though. Tall, reddish brown hair. Very pale."

Sorry, that ain't my Mark.

"He hasn't come into your life yet, but I see him very strongly. He will be very important to you. I can feel something now—much more powerfully. I see you becoming uncontrollably involved with this boy, which is very unlike you." She shook her head. "Is your current boyfriend important to you?"

She wanted to lie, but couldn't. "No. We just kind of hang out."

"That's also unlike you. You're independent. You don't follow fashion. You like crisp shirts and slacks for school, and you like to wear your hair in a braid down your back." June glanced at Cara. "Actually, I like your hair the way it is now."

"Thanks."

June briefly touched her fingers to her forehead. "There are so many images here. You're a complex young lady." Her own breathing quickened. "I see an injured man, a big man, overweight. His hip. It needs a replacement but he can't afford it and he's in pain. He's related to you."

"My dad," Cara said tightly. That was plain cruel.

"I see the man walking and—a car hits him. There's a lot of anger or—no, it's not anger. It's hatred, a terrible cold hatred—" She stopped. "I'm sorry, this is not right. It's nothing that affects you now."

"No, go ahead."

"A reading is not meant to scare you."

"I'm not scared," Cara said.

June seemed uncomfortable. "I was reading a very negative emotion, but it didn't make any sense. It wasn't vengefulness or spite, just an unthinking cruelty. It was coming from the driver of the car who hit your father."

"It was some drunk kid, they think," Cara said. "They never found him."

Pursing her lips, June considered. "I don't read intoxication." She exhaled. "But it's not helpful. I don't see the driver. And I see acceptance in your father. I see a closeness in your family. You're enraged at this accident. You don't like accidents. You want everything to make sense."

Cara kept chanting in her mind. *It's a prank. They told her all this.* But how much had she ever told Nancy? And would Nancy betray their friendship like this?

June seemed unsettled. "I see you at a party. It's going to take place soon, a few weeks from now. You're very involved with this party, planning it. It's a party for you—"

"My sweet sixteen."

"Cara," June said, "you don't have to prompt me."

"I wanted you to know you guessed right."

June said, "It's not guessing, sweetheart. And it's not important to let me know if I've gotten a 'right answer.' I keep losing the whole picture. I'm getting contradictory images, jangling sounds. I think you're fighting me very hard."

Cara's face grew warm. "I'm sorry. I'm being a jerk."

June rested her hands on her lap. "I see a slim, tall girl with long hair. You think she's set up this whole reading."

Cara moved to speak.

"Don't," June said. "Her name is Dyann, I think. She's shimmering in the air between us, in the forefront of your thoughts."

The air had grown stifling. "I don't like this," Cara said.

"Then I'll stop."

"No." Cara was trembling. "Go ahead. I want to know about the redheaded guy. The guy I'm going to fall in love with."

June gazed at Cara. "I can't tell you what your love life will be. I saw someone who might affect you deeply, but when this person appears you'll choose whether to let him into your life. Anyway, I don't see him now. I see other people you care about, friends from New York City."

"Huh?"

"Older friends," June said. "I see them very clearly. A girl especially, whom you looked up to. The girl has betrayed you. She's hurt you deeply, she's crushed your hopes—" Suddenly the room was silent. June's eyes half-closed. "These are not *your* friends, are they?"

Cara shook her head, scared now.

"You never lived in the city, you never met these people. They connect to someone who connects *with* you. Dyann. They're Dyann's friends. You're so closely woven together. She is urgently joined with your destiny. I've never experienced such closeness—it's like a single heartbeat.''

Cara felt sick. "What are you talking about? My best friend is Nancy Chu and she doesn't have any friends in the city."

Struggling for composure, June pressed her fingers to her lips. "I don't know that I should be telling you these things. There is not supposed to be negativity. Everything I tell you should be used in the most loving and constructive way."

"Why?" Cara demanded. "Life isn't all peaches and cream."

"Life is choices," June said emotionally. "A reading should be helpful, uplifting. It should inform you of your inner self, enough to help you make your life better."

"And my life isn't going to get better?"

June stood up and walked to the blinds. She opened them a slit and was wreathed in faint gray light. "I'm picking up very dark impressions, Cara, and they're not specific enough to help you. I read a shattering hatred that could hurt you very seriously."

Cara twisted around in the chair. "How?"

June looked back at Cara. "At your party I see colored lights spinning. Then I see the lights shatter, but I don't think it's a literal image. I think it's symbolic. And then I see darkness. I feel that hatred again, but I don't see you."

"What's that supposed to mean? Am I dead?"

"I don't know, Cara."

"Come on. The lights go out and you don't see me? Where did I go?"

June returned to her chair and sat down. "Listen to me, Cara. A psychic isn't a supernatural being. We're people with highly developed intuitive abilities. Sometimes I have a mystical awareness of things, and I can sense reality from outside myself. But it's not a game, and I can't tell you for certain what will happen."

"You see my death," Cara said softly. "And you don't want to tell me that."

"I see disturbing images. I see a car coming suddenly at people, and I see knives and spiders and Albany on a map, circled in red. I can't tell you what these images mean. I think they may be symbolic, but I don't want you to be unduly frightened."

"Too late. You have to give me something better than weird images."

"I can't." June looked totaled. "I can't tell you that you're going to die at your sweet sixteen party or before it, because I don't know that I've seen death."

"No," Cara said. "Just lights going out and nothingness."

"I'm so sorry." She leaned back, exhausted. "I've never had this happen." Stretching one arm to the table next to her, she shut off the cassette recorder. "I'd like you to come back. I want to do another reading. Maybe your initial hostility altered my perceptions. I want to see you again."

Cara stared at the cassette recorder. "I don't have enough money for that."

"There won't be any charge. I've never been troubled like this. If something has happened to my abilities, I need to know. Please come back, Cara.''

She nodded. ''Sure. Okay.''

''I'll keep the tape until then. This is not a proper reading.''

''Fine.'' She stood up, struggling not to puke. ''Any specific advice, like watch out for a falling piano?''

June managed a wan smile as she stood. ''No. Just take care of yourself. I don't think this is the story you wanted for your paper.''

''That's for sure.''

June walked her to the door and let her out. Cara watched as June shut the door, and a moment later she saw the blinds close. Standing in the cold drizzle, Cara hugged herself and shivered. *Idiot,* she scolded. *How could you let yourself be put through that?* She was going to tear Nancy's hair out.

She saw the car waiting, headlights on, and heard the thump of the stereo. She vaguely saw their faces through the streaked windshield. Even as she nurtured her anger, she knew that her life had changed forever.

CHAPTER
5

Nancy rang Cara's doorbell the next day and announced that she desperately needed to study for the chem test. This was a pretty obvious lie since Nancy could do chem standing on her head. But Cara let it go on for a few minutes, with Nancy perched on the edge of Cara's bed and Cara cross-legged on her carpet.

Finally Cara said, "Nancy, why did you really come here?"

"Why do you think I came over?"

"I can't guess."

"I want to know what happened yesterday!"

"With what?"

"With the *psychic!* Come on!"

Cara uncoiled and stood up, looking out her window at the trees. Were little tiny buds appearing—or just spots in front of her eyes?

"Cara, tell me," Nancy pleaded.

"I told you guys everything in the car."

"No way."

Cara dropped into the white secretary's chair by her desk. "I did. It was stupid."

"What did she really tell you?"

"That I was going to meet this mysterious red-headed boy and fall in love with him, and that something awful was going to happen at my sweet sixteen."

"There's got to be more than that."

"There isn't. I swear."

"So how come she kept the tape?"

Cara picked up a purple troll from her desk and turned it over in her hands. "I don't know. She probably didn't want me to sue her."

"Thea said her aunt *always* gives a client the tape, no matter what is on it."

"Well, she didn't give it to me."

Nancy shut the notebook next to her on the bed. "This is really a bummer, Cara. How could you not tell me more than you tell Dyann and Nick?"

Angrily, Cara asked, "How far do you want to take this, Nancy?"

"Huh?"

"You *know* you guys told June all that stuff about me, so you have to know what she said."

Nancy's voice was shaky. "You think we *told* her stuff?"

"Well, yeah. I figured that was the plan."

"You think I'd go along with that?"

"Don't throw a hissy fit, Nancy. You're not above pranking someone."

"Not *you*." Nancy really looked like she was going to cry.

"Okay, okay, forget I said anything."

Nancy stood up and started gathering her school stuff. "No, I can't forget you said that. It really sucks."

"Okay! Nancy! Calm down, I'm sorry."

Cradling her books to her chest, Nancy stood in Cara's doorway. "I don't know what Dyann did, or Nick, or Thea. But I wasn't part of it, and you really stink if you could believe that I'd tell her stuff about you behind your back."

Cara got up and went over to Nancy. "Look, this woman told me things about me that she couldn't possibly know unless someone told her. I don't believe she really *read* these things from my brain. So I drew an obvious conclusion."

"And included me."

Anger was mixing now with dread. "Well, Nancy, some of the stuff she said was stuff Dyann doesn't know and Nick doesn't know and Thea doesn't know."

"What stuff?"

"I don't remember all of it. About my dad's accident, and how Mark calls me Caramel and I call myself Mighty Mite and things about my personality that Dyann definitely doesn't know."

Nancy's eyes widened. She shifted the books in her arms. "She knew you were called Mighty Mite?"

"Nancy. Listen. I don't care if you pranked me. Just be honest. Did you tell this stuff to anybody?"

"No," Nancy said.

"You didn't give *any* information out?"

"I didn't tell anything," Nancy said emotionally. "I wouldn't screw you over, not for *those* jerks. Not for anybody."

Cara shook her head and draped her arms over her TV set. "So where did she get the information from?"

Nancy quietly put her schoolbooks down on Cara's bureau. "She's a psychic."

"Come *on!* Nobody can do that for real."

"How do you know?"

"They can't! How did she get into my brain and know what I call myself? How did she know about my dad, and my sweet sixteen party—"

"She knew about your party?"

"Yeah. And she knew there'd be a deejay because she saw colored lights." Cara thought furiously. "Okay, maybe I talked about that when Dyann was around, and Nick probably knows I'm having a party even though I'd invite Hitler before I'd invite him."

Nancy grinned.

"But none of those guys knows the other stuff. Unless they got it out of other people. I mean, I have other friends who know my dad was injured."

"Why would they tell that to Dyann or Nick?"

"Why not? Maybe they got money for it. Or maybe they just figured it was okay to pass on the information. It's not hard to get someone to tell you things."

Nancy sat on the bed again. "What about the pet names?"

Cara went to the window and watched the sky darken. "Well, Mark calls me Caramel, so he could have told them that."

"You think Mark would tell anything to *Dyann?*"

"Not Dyann, but Nick."

"Mark doesn't even know Nick."

"Okay, okay, so it doesn't make sense."

"And how many people know you call yourself Mighty Mite?" Nancy asked.

Cara tapped her fingernails on the window. "I don't know. I never counted."

"Oh, give it up. Almost nobody knows that. Maybe two people, and neither of them knows Dyann or Nick or Thea."

"Well, somebody told them." Cara faced Nancy. "I see Dyann behind all of this. She blames me for her editorial, and she probably blames me because she has no friends, so she wants to mess up my head. Somehow that wench got information about me and Thea got her aunt to go along and that's why June won't give me the cassette tape."

"But she said she wants you to come back," Nancy pointed out.

"She'll break the appointment. That's *my* prediction."

"And she didn't charge you."

Cara got up again and cleaned her papers off the rug. "Well, of course not. She was scamming me. She probably gave the tape to her niece, and Dyann and Nick are laughing right now." She slammed the papers down on her desk. "It makes me so mad!"

Nancy said, "You can't assume that."

"I can assume whatever I want," Cara said. "I've had it with Dyann and her moods. If she wants a better life let her ditch her attitude. And Nick can grow up too. I've got a paper to get out and schoolwork to do and a party to plan. I can't be bothered with games."

"Sounds okay to me," Nancy said. "So what do you want to do now?"

"Don't humor me," Cara said.

"Okay, drop dead."

They burst into laughter. Cara flopped stomach first onto the bed. "I will get past this. I just want it to be my birthday."

"And watch out for redheaded boys."

"Don't worry," Cara said.

Cara liked to sit alone in the stands. A warm wind sifted her hair, and the sun heated up her face. Best of all, nobody asked her questions.

The guys yelled a lot on the field as they played throw and catch. Mark whipped the ball to Joey Bianco along the first base line and once in a while he glanced up to where Cara sat. She smiled and waved. He looked pretty good down there; tight body, cute face.

She unwrapped a Twix bar she'd bought at lunch. The air felt so good. Winter had dragged on forever and this day was the first breath of spring. Cara tilted her head back and shut her eyes.

She heard the creak of somebody climbing the stands. Disappointment flooded her. *Not now.*

She opened her eyes and saw a strange guy. The sun was behind him so she couldn't see much except that he was dressed kind of preppy, with a light sweater and pressed jeans.

He walked up to her and said, "Seat taken?"

"No, but I think you have a lot of choices."

He chose to sit next to her. An odd sensation gripped her just under the ribs. He smiled at her, a shy smile. He was pretty good-looking, not drop-dead gorgeous, but she liked his light blue eyes, and the spray of freckles across his nose. His light brown hair blew freely.

"Hi," he said.

"Hi. Do I know you?"

"I don't think so. I don't go to this school."

"Oh." She wondered if she should feel scared, but Mike and the whole baseball team were only a scream away.

He spread his hands out on his knees and squinted at the action on the field. "I go to Lakehurst. I'm doing a story for the school paper."

"On the Westfield baseball team?"

"Yeah." He smiled again. "Our sports editor had the idea to do a piece about the opposition. How they practice, their strengths and weaknesses. Kind of clever, huh?"

"I guess so." Biting into the Twix bar, she said, "Wouldn't you wait until just before a game? They're not doing much now."

"Deadlines," he said. "Don't worry, I'm not a spy from the Lakehurst team."

"Wouldn't bother me," she said. "What's your name?"

"Danny," he said. "Danny Schonberg. You?"

"Cara Nelson."

He extended a hand and she reluctantly took it. He held her for a moment, then let go. "If you want to be alone, I'll move. I just thought it would be nicer to sit here with some company."

"Sit where you want," she said. She ate the Twix bar more rapidly and tried to keep her eyes on the field. It was hard not to be aware of him.

"I know you," he said.

"I don't think so."

"Well, I met you. You're the editor of the *Tempest,* right?"

"Yeah?"

"Columbia Scholastic Press Association. Newspaper competition, remember? Last May?"

She remembered the competition and meeting millions of other kids, but she didn't remember him. Then again, there was no way to be sure. "We met there?"

"Uh-huh. I asked you about how you did layout. No bells ringing?"

"Sorry." She finished the Twix and crumpled the wrapper, not wanting to ditch it under the seat while he was there.

"Well, I guess I don't make a good impression."

"You make a pretty good impression."

"Thanks." He stared intensely at her and she couldn't pull her eyes away. Finally he focused back on the field.

Cara took a deep breath. She knew what he was doing although she couldn't figure out why. If he'd liked her a year ago, how come he hadn't asked for her phone number then? Why hadn't he looked her up until now? Maybe he had a girlfriend and just broke up.

"So how do they look?" she asked, gesturing to the field.

"Out of practice."

She laughed. "Careful. My boyfriend is down there."

"Which one?"

"The guy near first base. Blond hair, white T-shirt."

"Throws pretty good."

"Yeah, he does."

He gazed at her steadily. "Did you ever look into someone's eyes and it took your breath away?"

"What?"

"I guess not."

"Maybe you should go," she said.

He stood up, hands in his pockets. "Sorry."

"What's this all about?" she demanded. "Is this some kind of joke?"

"No joke. Maybe I'll see you at the opening game."

"Yeah, great."

He gave her a little wave and walked away, not turning back. Cara faced front and said, "Huh!" Then she opened her palm and let the sticky Twix wrapper fall under the seat. The wind was colder and ice clouds drifted in front of the sun.

As she forced her eyes to find Mark, she thought that no boy had ever looked at her that way. Well, too bad for him. She was taken.

Not.

She stood up fiercely, standing against the wind. This was not supposed to happen.

Yes, it was.

Stop it. Don't even think about it.

Anyway, he wasn't a redhead. His hair was light brown.

Depending on how you saw it. He was in front of the sunlight. It could have been red hair.

That's exactly what people do. They twist everything to fit what the psychic said.

No way would she fall for it. He'd met her a year ago and now he was trying to hook up with her. He had *brown* hair, and he was gone. End of romance.

Slinging her canvas tote over her shoulder, she trudged down the bleacher seats. At field level she stopped and watched the guys. Mark was silhouetted by the sun, his movements unreal, like animated art. He cursed as he played, and he spat.

She made a grim face and moved toward him, to tell him she was going home.

CHAPTER
6

Dyann hunched over her desk, writing poetry on a lined yellow pad. She kept her room dim, shutters closed against fresh afternoon light.

"Dyann?" came her mother's voice from downstairs.

Dyann snapped upright and banged her pen down. "What?"

"Come down here for a moment, please."

"Coming." She yanked open her door and tumbled down the brief flight of steps. Mother waited on the couch, holding a sheet of paper.

"What?" Dyann asked.

Mother looked sternly at her. "Sit down, please."

Sighing, Dyann dropped into a wing chair. Mother wore the coral housedress she loved to put on after work. "This was in the mail today. It's an attendance letter from the high school. According to Mrs. Oslansky, you've been absent six times and cut twice."

"Oh God, Oslansky."

"What's that supposed to mean?"

"She's a witch and hates me."

Mother let the letter fall into her lap. "You were home sick twice this year. Every other day you went to school. How did you get six absences?"

"They were legal."

"Answer my question."

"I don't know."

"And the cuts?"

"I never cut."

"Is your teacher lying?"

Dyann scrunched up on the chair. "Ask her."

Mother shook the letter at Dyann. "If you want to hate me, fine, but you will not foul up in school."

"How do you know what I'm doing in school?" Dyann retorted. "Do you ever read anything I write? Do you ever ask me about my work?"

Mother said, "Don't try the injured child routine with me."

"That's what I am," she said and sulked.

"Maybe so, but it didn't happen here."

Furious, Dyann stood up. "Leave Father out of this."

Mother's eyes froze. "I've learned to deal with your fantasy of living with him."

"It's not a fantasy. Once I'm eighteen, I'm free."

"I know, you've told me. Until that time, I'm responsible for you, and you've been cutting classes and lying about absences. What did you do, pretend to be me on the phone?"

Dyann looked away. She hated being caught.

"Do you want to give me an answer?"

Dyann shrugged. "You have it all figured out."

Mother stood, holding the letter in her hand. "I am going to sign this and give it to you to take back. I'm also going to call the attendance office and ask them to call me when you're not in school. And you can plan on being grounded for the next two weeks."

"Who cares?" Dyann said. "I have nowhere to go anyway."

"Then you'll have time to make up the work you missed when you cut."

Looking up, Dyann said, "What?"

"I'm going to call Mrs. Oslansky and get assignments for you to do."

Dyann shot to her feet. "Why can't you just leave me alone?"

"No way, honey. You're mine."

"I'll never be yours. You can punish me until the end of time, but you'll never have me."

She rattled the door until it opened, then rushed outside. She thought she heard her mother yelling at her not to go out, but she blocked the words and slammed the door.

Cold wind swept around her, and she hugged herself against it. Head down, she walked along the concrete path between condos, listening to the rushing of wind in tree branches. Mother couldn't imagine the torture of each day in Westfield High School. Even the newspaper kids just barely tolerated her.

The only bright spot had been seeing Cara lose her cool. Dyann smiled briefly at the memory of Cara riding back in Nancy's car. Eddie was right. It felt good to play with that little snot's head.

A car's engine made Dyann turn toward it. She'd

been walking along the road that wound through the development. She saw a blue Camaro, slung low and driving beside her now. When she saw Mark Lanier and Joey Bianco inside, she snapped her eyes away.

The path back to her house was about fifty yards back. Pivoting, she began to walk fast. The car backed up beside her. "Nice butt," Mark yelled. "Pretty tight, though."

Fists clenched, she walked faster. Worse than their taunting was her fear of them. Mark's head was out the car window as he steered with one hand. "Come on in," he said.

"Get lost."

"You have something to say?"

Joey's voice added, "You got *nothing* to say."

The path was just ahead. Mark gunned the engine and she winced at the roar.

"Keep running," he said. "There's nowhere to go."

He pressed the horn and she stopped to look at them. "Haven't you had enough?"

Mark grinned. "Haven't even had a taste."

"Why don't you do this to Cara?" Dyann cried. "She printed the column."

Mark's face reddened a little. "You wrote it, you pay for it."

He sounded the horn again. Then he drove sharply away, tires screaming. Dyann stared at the fresh rubber marks on the faded asphalt.

Hating the idea of facing her mother, Dyann started back. She stopped when she saw a light green Monte Carlo across the road. It was an old car, with rust around the wheels and on the door. The car idled loudly and she thought that Eddie Belmonte was the driver.

Chest tight, she crossed the road. Yes, it was Eddie, his cap pulled down over his face. He leaned across the front seat and pushed open the door. Dyann slid in. The car smelled old and musty, like the windows had never been opened.

Eddie draped one arm over the steering wheel. "Don't quit the paper," he said.

A smile flickered across her lips. "Don't you ever do small talk?"

"Why?"

She crossed her arms tightly, feeling exposed. She saw only cap, sunglasses, and lips when she looked at him, and thought of the Invisible Man. It made her smile.

"You're happy now," he said.

"No."

"Best way to get them is to run the paper."

"Yeah. Extremely likely."

"How do you know what's likely?"

She pushed back her hair. "I know what my life is."

"No, you don't."

"What's the story, Eddie? Why is it so important for you to give me pep talks?"

"I like you."

She looked out the greasy window. "Don't do this."

"I think you're worth more than anybody in that school, but you bring yourself down."

"You sound like a guidance counselor."

He reached into a paper bag at his feet and drew

out a bottle of vodka. "It's about power. They try to make you think you can't have any. But you can get power. Just like they do."

"What are you talking about?"

"You got Cara to see June."

"Yes, so what?"

"Did it feel good?"

"For a few minutes."

He unscrewed the cap from the bottle, tilted it back and drank from it. "Why'd you stop?"

"Why did I stop what?"

"You made her do what you wanted. She got scared."

"That was because of what June said. I didn't plan that."

"Part of winning is what you plan, part of it's what you don't."

She uttered a small laugh. She'd told him what Cara said about June's reading. She remembered how quietly he listened.

"Eddie, I wish you could come to Manhattan with me. You'd like the city."

"I've been there." He held the bottle toward her.

She wanted it, but fear held her back. "I've got to go. If I stay out too long I'll be punished forever."

"You let it happen," he said.

"I have no choice!" She glared at him. "You want me to play all these games, but it doesn't do any good. It won't stop those idiots from tormenting me, and it won't stop Cara from running the newspaper, and it won't stop my mother from keeping me prisoner. I don't know what you want from me, Eddie."

He said, "I want to put you on top."

"It won't happen."

"It's happening."

"*How*, Eddie? Give me some details. Where do I get this outrageous power?"

"Seize the advantage."

The fumes from the idling engine were giving her a headache. She needed him. With Myra gone, with Daddy gone, he was the only promise she had.

Overpowered by her feelings, she moved toward him. Her fingers dug into the folds of his trench coat. She kissed him hard. He allowed the kiss, but gave nothing back.

She recoiled, feeling sick. "Why did you do that?" he asked.

"I don't know." Her voice cracked. "I thought it's what you wanted."

"Think about what *you* want."

She took the bottle from him, wrapped both hands around it. "I don't understand you."

"Seize the advantage," he repeated.

"I don't have any advantage." Shutting her eyes, she drank hard, forcing the clear liquor down her throat. She gagged, and it burned. Her breath came raggedly, and she drank again.

"Do what you want," he said.

"Yeah." She thrust the bottle back at him. "I'll see you, Eddie."

She bolted from the car and shut the door hard. The wind chilled her damp skin as she scurried across the road. The vodka swam in her brain and she hated herself.

*   *   *

That night Cara and Nancy trudged toward Cara's house down Hobart Avenue, hugging the edges of lawns. No sidewalks made night walks a little risky.

Bundled in school jackets, they laughed and chatted. Cara held a paper sack.

"More chips," Nancy demanded.

"Come on," Cara complained. "We'll have none for the house."

"I need chips to give me energy."

Nancy bumped Cara with her hip and Cara bumped back. Then Nancy clawed at the bag. Cara squealed *"No!"* and giggled. They battled over the bag, skipping into the center of the dark road and back toward the edges of lawns.

The chips were for a party-planning session. This night the exalted few would be chosen to attend Cara's sweet sixteen. Cara liked the bubbles of excitement she felt. She'd mostly shaken off June's dark predictions and even her meeting with Danny.

"You finish Graham's paper yet?" Nancy asked.

"Nope. You?"

"Nope."

That brought more giggles. Tree branches moved in the light breeze. A car's headlights suddenly blinded them and they skipped back to the side of the road. The car swept past.

"Just run us over," Cara said. "Don't bother to ask."

"Quiet night," Nancy said.

"Yeah. It really feels like springtime. You can smell it."

They sniffed deeply and Cara screwed up her nose. *"Eeeeuuuuu!"*

"Dog poop!" Nancy cried.

Cara laughed hysterically. They resumed their walk and Cara listened to her sneakers crunching on the road.

"You and Mark still fighting?" Nancy asked.

"I don't know what we're doing. He used to be funny and cool, and now it's like he plays the stupid jock all the time."

Nancy munched a chip. "Too complicated."

Cara tried to shake the blues. She concentrated on the closeness of Nancy and good feelings about the party. Cara glanced at a brightly lit house. "Look at that bird in there."

Nancy looked. It was teal and gold and sat in a huge white cage by the window. "Looks like a macaw."

The bird screeched so loudly that Cara yelped. They laughed and clung to each other. "I'd say he sounds totally rude," Cara said.

Hearing a car behind them, Nancy said, "Watch out."

Cara fell in line behind Nancy. She saw Nancy's jeans illuminated by the headlights and heard the car's engine. "So pass us already," she said.

She twisted her head and saw the headlights. "What's with that guy?"

"I don't know but let's walk fast."

"Good idea." They quickened their pace and the car stayed behind them. Cara's throat crimped. "I don't like this."

"If anyone gets out," Nancy said, "run for the nearest house."

But the car stopped and the engine sound got farther and farther away as the girls walked. Cara let out a long breath. "He must have been looking for an address."

"As long as he wasn't looking for me," Nancy said.

Cara worked on calming her pounding heart. She wished they were in her den.

The engine roared behind them, and the driver flicked on his brights. Cara stopped breathing and turned around. She realized the car was moving.

"He's coming after us."

"Move!"

The car was on top of them. Cara stared at it, paralyzed. At the last second she flung herself into the brush and the car rocketed past.

Cara half lay in the brush, unable to stop trembling. She smelled damp rotting leaves. Nancy was crying a few feet away. "Stupid jerk," Cara yelled.

She stood up, brushing twigs and leaves from her jacket. Nancy stood nearby, hugging herself. Cara looked around for the bag, but didn't see it. "There goes our snack food."

"Forget it," Nancy said. "Let's just get to your house."

"Good thinking." She spat out shreds of foliage and felt a burning sensation over her right eye. Great. She was probably cut and it would probably need stitches. "I can't believe that idiot."

As she brushed off the knees of her jeans, she heard Nancy cry out, *"Cara!"*

Headlights slammed onto her. She screamed and turned. The car veered toward her, thumping over fallen logs. Cara ran wildly as the car pursued her. She saw the lighted house, the house with the bird.

She could feel the heat from the car's engine. She ran up on the driveway of the house and dove onto the lawn, rolling behind a pair of big yews. The car spun back onto the road and raced up the street toward Miller Road.

In the abrupt silence, Cara heard her own breathing. It was horrible, like an animal dying. She threw up on the grass. Inside the house the bird squawked again, but nobody came out.

Cara forced herself to calm down. *Come on, you're okay. Fortunately, he couldn't hit such a small target.*

She pushed up on her hands and knees and rocked back and forth, testing for broken bones. Cautiously, she stood and peered up and down the road. No car.

"I see a car coming suddenly at people—"

They were like words on a tape, and they rattled Cara with terror. "Shut up!" she hissed. She had to get control back. She had to get home and feel her carpet and see her stuffed animals and taste corn chips and know that her life was still normal.

She walked back toward where Nancy had been but didn't see her. "Nance? Are you okay? Nance?"

Moaning came from the brush. Nearly fainting with dread, Cara rushed over and searched the darkness. She saw Nancy lying on her side, face half in dead leaves. Her eyes shimmered.

"Oh God, are you okay? What happened?"

"I don't know," Nancy said. "I think my leg's broken."

Cara knelt down and even in darkness could see

the flap of denim hanging and the ghastly slash of white bone against dark blood. Puke came up in her throat again but she forced it down. "Just stay there," she said. "I'll get someone."

She turned and walked away, unable now to stop the brimming of tears in her eyes or the sobs that shook her.

CHAPTER
7

As Cara sat on the living room couch, she wished that she and Nancy had never gone to the 7-Eleven. Her forehead throbbed with a bruise that was blowing up by the minute. She still hadn't changed out of her grungy clothes. And now she thought she was going to puke again.

From the kitchen, Cara could hear her dad and the cop who'd arrived about ten minutes ago. Glancing to her right, she saw the whirling red light on the driveway. Those lights always scared her.

Mom returned from the bathroom, with a washcloth draped across her hands. "Here," she said. "Lie back and keep this on your head."

"I can't lie back anymore," she said. "It gets me sick."

"Cara, come on. You'll look like Frankenstein if that lump gets any bigger."

Sighing, Cara leaned back against the flowered

cushions. Mom sat next to her and gently spread the washcloth across her forehead. The fire cooled, and she felt her eyes shutting, but that made everything spin, so she forced them open.

Mom stroked her sticky hair. "This is really crazy," she said.

Cara looked up at Mom. "I'm so sorry. You and Dad were supposed to go out tonight."

"Don't worry about it."

"But I messed up your evening."

Mom smiled. "Children always mess up their parents' evenings."

Her voice caught and she bit her lip. Cara sat up and hugged her. The washcloth fell to her lap but she didn't care. She just hung onto Mom and let her body shake with crying.

Then it was over and Cara fell back again. Mom picked up the washcloth, but Dad and the cop came in so she just folded it up and held on to it.

"How are you doing?" Dad looked scared.

"Fine, Daddy," she said.

"You look lousy."

She could tell he was really shook up. "Just cuts and scratches."

"Yeah, well, we're going to the emergency room."

"No, Daddy!"

"It's not your choice."

She sighed. The cop was young and kind of cute. For a second she thought of Danny, but pushed the image back down. The cop said, "Are you sure you can't give me any description of the car?"

"I just saw the stupid headlights," she said.

"Okay," the cop said. "I doubt there's anything

we can do. Without a license plate number or the make and model of the car, there's nothing to investigate. It was probably some drunk or some kids who thought this would be funny."

"Some joke," Cara said. "Nancy's in the hospital and I'm a mess."

The cop looked at her with sympathy. "Most hit and runs don't get caught. If you remember anything, call the precinct." He flipped his report pad closed. "We'll check with the Chu girl to see if she remembers anything. I hope you feel better."

"Thanks," Cara said. She watched her dad walk the cop to the front door. The neighbors would have a great time tonight wondering what was going on.

Hatred. That's what June had read. A terrible, cold hatred in whoever hit Daddy. Cara had felt hatred when the car chased her. She wondered how Nancy was doing. She remembered the ambulance coming and Nancy being strapped onto a stretcher and shoved inside, like a pizza being shoved into an oven.

Cara punched the couch and her eyes filled again. She ached to tell Mom and Dad about the psychic's reading, but it would sound so stupid.

Mom came back and sat down again. "Come on, sweetie. I'll help you change into something clean and we'll take a ride to the hospital."

"We don't have to," Cara insisted. "I'm okay. It's just bumps and bruises."

"I know, but there could be internal injuries. Even if there's nothing, it pays to get checked out."

Dad said, "We'll stop for ice cream on the way back."

Mom glared at him. "Maybe it would be best to put her to bed after this."

"Whatever she wants," Dad said, crestfallen.

"I want ice cream," Cara said.

Cara let Mom help her up. She swayed for a moment as dizziness swirled through her head. Then she said, "I'm okay."

"I hope so," Mom said.

When they got back from Friendly's, Mark's blue Camaro waited in the driveway. Mom said, "Cara, look who's here."

From the backseat, Cara said, "He must have called and didn't get an answer."

"Very loyal," Mom said. "But I don't want him to stay long. You need sleep. Besides, you've got medication in you."

"Don't worry," Cara said. "I'm not in the mood for passion."

Dad made a rude noise as he pulled up alongside the front lawn. "Tell him to move his car so I can get into the garage."

"Calm down, Daddy," Cara said. "Look, he's doing it already."

She watched out the window as Mark pulled back and swung into the road. The headlights struck her eyes and for a second, she saw the oncoming car again, and nearly screamed. Dad backed up and pulled onto the driveway. Mom pressed the remote for the garage door opener and the door lifted slowly. Cara said, "I'll be two minutes," as she got out of the car.

Walking turned out to be a little tough. Mark stood

by his car door, worried. "What the hell happened to you?"

"Someone tried to run me down," she said.

"No way! I heard that cop cars were here and I came over but the house was locked."

"Mom and Dad took me to the emergency room."

"This is sick," Mark said. He seemed really shaken. "Are you sure you're okay?"

"Yeah, I'm okay. It's good to see you."

Emotion flooded her and he grabbed her at the same time. She held him desperately as he stroked her hair and back. The sobs kept coming and coming, while he kept saying, "Shh, it's okay, it's okay."

Finally the sobbing subsided. "Just hold me," she whispered.

"Yeah, no problem."

She rested her cheek against his rough jacket and felt the night wind on her face. "The car hit Nancy. Her leg's broken."

"Who was this clown? He's a dead man."

"I didn't see the driver. I don't even know what kind of car it was. Probably some drunk."

Mark got very quiet and stopped rubbing her back. Cara leaned back in his arms and searched his face. He stared at her.

"What's the matter?" she asked.

His eyes looked tormented, as if he were trying to decide something. Finally he said, "Do you hang out with Dyann a lot?"

"Not much. I see her at newspaper meetings."

"Keep away from her."

Cara stepped back. "What are you talking about?"

He looked down and rubbed his nose. "Forget it. I'm not talking about anything."

"You're talking about *something*. What's up?"

Grabbing her arms, he pulled her close and said, "Look, we've been giving her a hard time."

"Who?"

"Me and some of the other guys."

She should have been angry about this, but her head was so jangled that she couldn't even make sense of it. "What were you doing?"

"Nothing violent," he said hastily. "I mean, she probably made it a big deal when she told you, but we just harassed her."

"How?"

This was tough for him. "We said stuff to her in class. Yesterday, we went to her development and she was walking outside, so we hazed her a little."

Now the anger came up. "What kind of hazing?"

"Nothing bad."

She tore his hands away. "You couldn't stand it that I wouldn't sack her and that Mr. Brill wouldn't sack her so you decided to intimidate her into quitting."

"Yeah, pretty much." Now his voice was edged with anger. "I told you, we didn't want her on the paper anymore."

"Except it wasn't your decision." She crossed her arms over her chest. "You creep. No wonder she hates my guts."

"That's the problem," Mark said.

"What's the problem?"

"Listen! She's a total weirdo. I mean, she doesn't

talk to anybody except Thea who's weird also, and she doesn't like anybody.''

"Mark, what is this leading to?"

With a piercing stare, he said, "I'm just worried she might take it out on you."

Cara stared at him, trying not to laugh. He looked so serious standing there. "You think Dyann tried to run me down tonight?"

"I know it sounds stupid."

"Well, yeah, it does sound stupid."

"But you don't really know her, right?"

She wrapped her arms around him and kissed him, too unexpectedly for him to respond. "I think it's beautiful that you care this much."

He hugged her back. "I told you I care."

"I don't think Dyann is the type to go running people down, but how about if you and your friends lay off her? Then I won't be in danger."

"I still don't like her on the paper."

"But you want me alive, right?"

"Right."

"So give her a break and she won't kill me."

"I'm keeping my eye on her."

"Okay, as long as you keep your hands off her."

This time they were both ready for the kiss, and she let it go on and on. She threw her whole heart into loving him, pressing her fingers against his hard back. The wind hummed in her ears.

But when they stopped and held each other quietly, she sensed the hollowness of her feelings. She saw Danny's face and experienced a painful yearning that made no sense, but was there anyway. Underneath lay a crippling dread. Her sixteenth birthday was in a couple of weeks and she didn't want to die.

"Hey," Mark whispered. "Are you going to be okay?"

She nodded.

"How about I come in for a while."

She shook her head. "No. I'm wiped out."

"Okay. I'll call you tomorrow."

"Thanks, Mark."

He ruffled her hair. "It's okay, Caramel."

She watched him get into his car and drive away as she stood on the driveway, shivering. *I wish I loved you,* she thought sadly. She felt the medication turning her brain into foam and nothing mattered now except getting to sleep.

The next afternoon Cara went to the newspaper office, figuring she'd see what had come in, and write some of the articles herself if she had to. She felt like doing this about as much as she felt like skydiving, but the paper had to make the deadline. Right then she resented the responsibility she usually embraced. She just wanted to go home and go to sleep.

Cara noticed that the lights were on in the *Tempest* office. She thought instantly of Danny, but brushed the thought aside. She tiptoed to the door and peeked in. "Hello?"

Dyann sat at a small desk, with a pile of papers in front of her. She looked up. "Oh, hi, Cara. How are you?"

"Pretty good. What's happening?"

Dyann had covered her flowing hair with a cap. "I

was just going through the stories in the folder and revising them."

"Oh. I was going to do that."

"I didn't mean to take anything away from you. I just realized that we were getting closer to deadline and I knew you'd been hurt."

Cara dropped her schoolbag on the counter near the LASERWRITER and sat down. "No it's okay. Thanks."

Dyann smiled. "Are you any better?"

"I'm fine, just banged up." Her pulse quickened. Dyann couldn't be this cool about attempted murder.

"What about Nancy?" Dyann asked as her pen darted to a loose-leaf page.

"Broken leg." Cara tapped her fingernails on a desk. This wasn't easy. Cara was used to comforting people when they had problems, and advising people when they had to do something painful. Now she was the one who needed comfort and advice.

"Listen," she said. "Mark told me about what he's been doing."

"Oh." Dyann sat back.

"I'm really sorry. I told him what I thought of him."

"Are you still going out with him?"

Cara's chest clenched. "Dyann, I'm trying to apologize. You always make it so hard."

Dyann lowered her eyes. "I don't mean to make it hard, Cara. I was just curious about whether you'd keep dating someone like that."

"He's not 'someone like that,' " Cara said heatedly. "He's not the brightest guy in the world, but he's not evil. He went along with his friends."

"The Nuremberg defense."

"All right, forget it," Cara said. "I just thought I'd tell you."

"I appreciate it."

Dyann went back to her revising. Somehow, it annoyed Cara that she was doing it. Yet Cara was grateful because the task would be finished. She couldn't deal with these conflicting emotions. She really had to go home and go to sleep.

She stood, and her rage at Dyann swelled. She blurted, "Dyann, what kind of car do you drive?"

"Huh?"

"Someone said you drove a Trans Am, and I said no way. What do you drive?"

Tapping her knuckles with her pen, Dyann said, "Cara, I don't even have a license."

Great, she thought. *You just made a total ass of yourself.* "Well, I guess that person didn't know what he was talking about."

"Guess not."

Cara yanked her schoolbag off the counter and slung it over her shoulder. "Don't go crazy with this stuff. I'll do it tomorrow."

"It's okay. I don't mind."

"Well, I can't help you. I've got to sack out."

With an encouraging smile, Dyann said, "Go ahead. I'm fine here. I'll lock up."

"Okay. Thanks."

Cara turned and left the office. Her head throbbed as she trudged down the stairs. She knew, before thinking about it, that she was going to call June. What she really wanted to know about was Danny. Already, Cara was planning to go over to Lakehurst High School to check him out.

CHAPTER

8

June said, "I feel terrible about last time, Cara. I didn't mean to scare you like that."

"You didn't scare me," Cara said. "What *happened* scared me."

"I can imagine. What a horrible experience."

"Well, you predicted it."

The words stung. "Cara, you must stop thinking that I make predictions. I can see down roads you might take. But I can't tell you what will happen."

"You did," Cara said. "You told me I'd meet a redheaded boy and I did, and you told me you saw a car coming at people." She twined her hands in her lap. "I didn't believe in psychics before I came here, but this is pretty impressive."

June's heart went out to the child. Beneath her assertiveness, there was self-doubt and loneliness. Her carefully constructed world could be shattered easily.

June leaned back in her chair. "The car I saw could have been the one that struck your father. And as a teenage girl, you meet lots of young men. Besides, you said this fellow had brown hair."

"Light brown," Cara insisted. "You could call it red, I guess."

"No, *you* could call it red. And drunks run people down every day. This could have been a coincidence."

Cara's eyes beseeched June. "You're trying to make me feel better," she said.

"Definitely."

"But you're lying!" Cara snapped. "You're going back on everything you said."

"You're being pert, Cara."

"I'm being honest. Maybe you don't like *my* reading."

June stood up and walked to the bookshelves that lined her wall. Knowing she was avoiding Cara's eyes, she concentrated instead on her hand. Her skin looked old. Oh, well. What was middle age without crisis?

"June?" Cara said. "Are you going to help me?"

Are you? June asked herself. She turned to face Cara. "I'm not sure I can. If someone truly tried to kill you—"

"There's no if," Cara said. "He chased us and then he turned around and came after us again."

"Well, then, it's a police matter."

"The police won't do anything. I can't describe the car. I can't give them a license. That's why I came to you."

"I can't see the car if you didn't," June lied. She

could see the car right then, hanging in the air like a hologram.

"But you can see feelings, and you can see people who hate me. Read my mind, June. My best friend has a broken leg. This guy *hit* her! He could have killed me right there. He just didn't want to. But maybe he'll want to next week, or the week after. I can't live like that, not knowing."

June's hand trembled on the bookshelf. All the images came flooding back—the green map with the red circle, the scuttling of thousands of spiders, colored lights spinning so fast they made her sick. Driving all of the images was a hatred that burned her lungs.

"I feel for you," she said. "I just can't give you the answers you want."

"Why not?" Cara asked.

"I don't have them."

"You do have them. You won't tell me."

Rankled, June said, "Cara, I don't like being interrogated. Just like a doctor, I have ethics, and my ethics limit what I can tell a client."

"Like I'm going to die?"

"Exactly."

"A doctor tells you if you're going to die."

June stood behind her chair, hands clutching the back. "No, a doctor tells you that you've contracted a disease that will probably be fatal given the available data. I see images, Cara. I see possible pathways in your life, but I can't identify a virus or prescribe a course of treatment."

"You can tell me what you see. You can tell me what to watch out for."

June suddenly despised her gifts as she imagined

being interviewed on television. "Yes, I saw the murder, it was such a strong, evil image." *Why didn't you warn her?* "We're not supposed to upset our clients." *But you knew—you knew it would be in a car, you knew it would be in Albany, you knew it would be the redheaded—*

"Albany?" Cara said. "What about Albany?"

Damn it. She'd been vocalizing. She came around the chair and sat. "I told you last time, I saw an image of Albany on a map, circled in red. I don't know whose map it is. Do you have relatives or friends upstate?"

"No," Cara said. "My older sister is in Virginia and my brother goes to school out in Oregon."

"I don't see the threat of people running from a car, not any longer."

"Well, it already happened."

"Try not to interrupt." June coldly pushed away her doubts. She was going to do what she had to do. "I see you going on a car trip sometime in the near future. It may be to Albany, I'm not sure. I see you in a van with this boy Danny, but again, I don't know if you're going to Albany or somewhere else. I see this happening after your sweet sixteen party."

She heard Cara's intake of breath. "Then I'm going to live past the party!"

"Cara, I never said you weren't."

"You saw all that darkness, *at* the party."

"The darkness is a feeling, not a literal prediction. I still sense a disturbing hatred, and it's connected with you. But it may be the hatred of whoever struck your father. It may be someone close to you. This girl Dyann is very angry with you, but the hatred doesn't emanate from her.''

"I didn't think she'd try to run me over.''

"She is nevertheless strongly linked to you. I can feel her fear, I can sense her trying to run from someone.''

"Maybe it's my boyfriend,'' Cara prompted. "Mark admitted that he was harassing Dyann.''

"That may be it,'' June said. "In fact, all of this may be nothing more than normal teenage crisis.''

"Not Mr. Hit and Run,'' Cara said. "And what about the spiders and knives?''

"I still sense them,'' June admitted. "That answer may be fears that lie deep within you, fears stemming from your childhood. You once put your hand down on a big spider, while you were digging in your backyard.''

Cara's eyes widened. "Yes. I was about seven. Oh God, I still remember that. It was so gross.''

"You weren't supposed to be digging there, either.''

"No.'' She smiled. "Mom told me never to go there, that I'd get ticks. I did get a tick once.''

"So the spider made a strong impression.'' June smiled. "When I see darkness, Cara, I can be seeing many things. That's why I can't 'predict' your death or your romantic life. You wanted me to answer all the questions, to deal with all your fears. But *you* have to do that. It's your life.''

Cara slumped back in the leather chair, feeling tiny and lost in it. "I guess I just got freaked out by that car.''

"I'd get freaked out too.'' She stood up to signal

the end of the interview. "You're all so intense these days. My niece, Thea, too. It's hard to be a kid."

Cara stood up then. "That's for sure."

June clasped her hands in front of her. "Cara, you're a strong-self-directed young lady. You have intelligence and maturity beyond your age. Don't let this incident spook you. Enjoy your party and enjoy whatever romance comes your way."

Cara's smile was fleeting. "Thanks. I guess I was a little whacked."

June put a reassuring hand on the girl's shoulder as she saw her out. When Cara had gone, June leaned against the door and shut her eyes. *It's not your responsibility,* she thought savagely. But the images played out in her tormented mind. June envisioned the redheaded boy, and felt the evil in him. His cheeks bulged and spiders suddenly scuttled out of his mouth. His eyes reddened. His hand clutched an impossibly long knife. Cara's mouth opened in a silent scream.

No more. The girl had to work out her own destiny. And Thea would have to be lectured about bringing any more friends to her aunt.

Dyann stood over Thea as she worked on a story for the *Tempest.* "Almost done?"

Thea nodded. Her thin shoulders hunched as she concentrated.

"Good." Dyann enjoyed the warmth of the afternoon sun through the window. Nick intently typed on one of the MACs. Dyann watched him peer at the screen and smiled.

She wandered to the doorway of the classroom and

gazed out at the empty corridor, half hoping to see Eddie. Eddie wouldn't visit, not if he knew other people were there. Still, she allowed a wistful ache in her chest.

"Dyann!" It was Nick's voice.

She turned. "Yes?"

Nick pushed a hand through his unruly hair and looked down at the page he'd printed out. "Are you sure we want to run the story like this?"

"Which story?"

"The sports story." He read in a quick monotone. " 'Spring traditionally brings hope for rebirth and growth, but for the Westfield baseball and lacrosse teams, it brings despair.' " He looked up. "That's pretty rough."

"Is it true?"

Nick thought about it. "I guess it is. They both lost their first games—"

"They were wiped out, and from what the coaches and the players say, it won't get better."

Nick stared at her. "Yeah, but a lot of this is just what people are saying, not anything official."

Dyann threw an arm around Nick, who looked startled. "Official means write only nice, upbeat, inspiring things. This is why you find all the copies of the *Tempest* on the floor."

She squeezed Nick's shoulder and sat down at a desk where she'd set out other stories. Nick followed her. "The jocks are going to freak over this."

"News is news."

"What if they come after *me?* My name's going on it."

"If you're worried, put my name on it."

"Really? Can I?"

She smiled at him. "Go right ahead. I like the attention."

"You're a nut job," Nick said. "And how come you're in charge of this issue anyway?"

"Cara's recovering," Dyann said, "or something."

"So why aren't I taking over? I was up for editor-in-chief."

Dyann violently scribbled out an entire passage, her hair falling over the paper. "Nick, you didn't even write the stories you were supposed to write, and you didn't get the articles from the reporters you were assigned. If you have to know, I asked Mr. Brill if he wanted me to help out with this issue, and he said yes."

"You mean you kissed up."

Dyann tossed her hair and made kissing noises. Nick cursed and stormed away.

Thea stared at this scene; Dyann caught her eye and laughed. Thea looked down quickly. The sun felt exceptionally warm on Dyann's back. As she worked, she grew more excited. If she could just get this issue out, she could take the *Tempest* away from Cara. And, in charge of the paper, she could destroy Cara's boyfriend. She'd make sure Nick got all the names in the stories, so everyone could read about Westfield's goats—even college scouts.

Dyann looked over at Thea. "How's it going, babe?"

"Okay." Thea cast her eyes down and seemed to shrink inside her green coat.

"You're good, Thea. I might make you news editor."

Thea stiffened. "Cara's the editor-in-chief."

"For the moment." Seeing how horrified Thea appeared, Dyann said, "And anyway, she'll appreciate what you did to get this issue to press."

"I don't get to lead anything." Thea's voice broke as she returned to her work. Dyann could almost taste the girl's depression. Thea lived in shadows, a nervous mouse who'd never be sexy or popular. How well Dyann knew the feeling. But winning wasn't impossible. *Try it, Thea. Try crawling out of your cave and sitting in the sun.*

Dyann swore that Eddie stood at the door. She hurried into the hall. Dust seemed to rush past her. He'd been there. He'd always be there, for her. With clawed fingers, she raked the doorjamb and hurt with her need for him.

CHAPTER

9

Cara slumped in her desk in health class and watched Mr. Haller try to lecture while Eddie Belmonte drove him nuts. Eddie always drove Mr. Haller nuts. You could see Mr. Haller's eyes get wild as he watched Eddie, even though he kept talking.

"Saturated fat!" Mr. Haller yelled. He paused dramatically, then whirled and scrawled the words on the blackboard. Then he whirled back again, the chalk still in his hand. "Saturated fat is made from *animal organs!* It's the *worst fat you can eat!* It's *solid!* It *raises* your blood cholesterol!" He whirled again and scrawled RAISES CHOLESTEROL on the board.

Some kids giggled at his wildness. Others had their heads down on their desks. It was a heads-down day; warmer than it had been, with the sun pounding through the big windows.

"Eddie, get your feet off the desk," Mr. Haller

said. Cara doodled in her notebook, fighting a headache. The Mighty Mite had run out of gas. All she wanted now was for the day to end so she could go home and take a nap.

Amazing how that stupid car had affected her. Two nights ago her mom had asked her to walk three houses down to return a frying pan. Every time she heard a car or saw headlights coming up a side street, she froze and her insides shook. She ran home and sat on her bed hugging her knees for twenty minutes.

Clunk. Clunk. Eddie's feet were down. Mr. Haller rattled the chalk around in his closed hand and paced back and forth. "Some saturated fats do *not* come from animals. They are *tropical* and *hydrogenated vegetable oils!*" He whirled again and scrawled TROP. & HYDR. VEG. OILS.

A low snickering told Cara that Eddie's feet were up again. Her chest tightened at the coming conflict. Mr. Haller whirled and *wham!* his eyes fixed on Eddie. Cara looked down. "Belmonte, you are the world's biggest waste!"

Wincing, Cara drew furious little cartoons. Mr. Haller strode to the back of the room. The class was a lost cause now. It was Haller and Belmonte, one on one for the rest of the period.

Cara shifted around to see. Eddie sat in his usual position, with that stupid smirk on his face. Not that she could see his face behind the cap and shades. She stared at one humongous boot sole that faced her from its perch on his desk. Haller loomed over him, shaking with rage.

"Get them down," he commanded.

Eddie kept writing in his folder.

"Last time."

Eddie kept writing.

Mr. Haller slapped the folder from Eddie's hands. It fell to the floor and papers scattered.

"Get them down!"

Eddie snickered. Mr. Haller's hands clamped around Eddie's leg.

"Get your hands off me," Eddie said.

Cara's heart froze.

"Get your damn legs down."

"Get your hands off me."

Mr. Haller yanked Eddie's leg off the desk and pushed it down. Eddie threw his desk over and sprang up, shoving Mr. Haller. *"I said get your hands off me."*

The kids were going crazy. Half of them had left their seats and circled the two antagonists. Some were shouting. Cara held on to the edge of her desk.

Mr. Haller just stood there, breathing so hard Cara thought he'd have a heart attack. Eddie faced him. In the flowing trench coat, you couldn't tell how ready he was to fight. Cara knew Eddie had been suspended a zillion times, so he probably didn't care.

"No," Mr. Haller said in a hoarse voice. "No way do you get *me* in trouble. I get *you* in trouble. You are a piece of crap. You are getting out of my class."

Eddie smirked again. "I gotta take health. State says so."

"Not here." He whirled and stormed to the front of the room. Cara could almost feel wind as he passed. The other kids wandered back to their seats, laughing and talking. Mr. Haller furiously yanked open a desk drawer and pulled out a pad of hall passes.

Cara suddenly noticed that someone had come into the room. It was a student, one of the office helpers. Cara knew this by the laminated tag that hung from her belt. She held a small gift-wrapped box.

A kid in the class yelled out, "Mr. Haller, someone's here."

This brought more laughter. Mr. Haller glared at the girl. "Yes?"

The girl thrust the box at him. "This is for Cara Nelson."

Mr. Haller looked at Cara. "Cara, it's for you."

She got up and took the box. The girl fled from the room. Cara held the box stupidly, trying to make sense of it. Mr. Haller said, "You can sit down again, Cara."

Cara said, "Oh. Yeah."

Cara looked at Eddie before she returned to her seat. He was perched on the radiator, his dark form haloed by the bright window. She swore he was looking at her.

She lowered her eyes. His folder was still on the floor. She saw a map sticking out of it, and her stomach lurched. She couldn't see what place the map represented, but she swore there were red circles on it.

"Over here, Eddie," Mr. Haller said. The words made Cara jump.

Eddie got off the radiator and scooped up the folder, stuffing its contents back in. Before Cara could get out of his way, he skimmed past her, the flaps of his trench coat slapping her legs.

Cara stared at the floor where the folder had been, then stumbled back to her seat. A map with red circles. It made sense. Eddie was always writing in that folder. Somehow, she'd seen the map, or seen him making the red circles, and that's what June saw in her mind.

So much for spiders and maps.

But that meant everything was logical and Danny wasn't meant for her and she'd probably never see him again. Unless she went after him. Except that she had a boyfriend and she couldn't cheat on Mark. Only if it was *destined*. Astonished, she realized how much she wanted the magic to be real.

The nerves in her hands sent a message to her brain: *package here, dimwit!* With a jolt, she looked at the box. There was a small envelope stuck in the yellow ribbon, with her name on it. Mr. Haller was handing the pass to Eddie. Cara tore open the envelope and slipped out the folded loose-leaf paper. She glanced up. Mr. Haller and Eddie were at the door. She unfolded the paper and read it.

> *Hi. I keep missing you. Would you meet me at the front entrance of Lakehurst at 2:45? I want to talk for a while. I know this is stupid, but I can't get you out of my mind. Just talk. Promise. Danny.*

Her heart pounded so hard she was sure everyone could hear it. She folded up the note and, with shaking hands, unwrapped the box and lifted the lid. Inside was a troll doll with a dunce cap. Cara took it out of the box. A luggage tag was affixed to it, with the handwritten words, *I'd make a fool of myself for you*.

Cara stared at the troll. Then voices intruded. "Wow, what is it?" "Who gave you that? Mark?" "Let me see!"

Really wise, opening this right in the middle of the classroom. She cradled the troll and faked a smile for the girls who crowded around her. "It's a troll doll," she said, trying desperately to figure out how to break off the tag.

Mr. Haller said, "Class back in session. Everyone in your seats. We *are* going to have a lesson."

Thank you, Mr. Haller! Cara stuffed the troll doll back into the box, along with the note from Danny, and slid it under her seat. She'd have to call home and leave a message on the machine so Mom would know she'd be late. Then she'd take the Number 12 bus, which passed within six blocks of Lakehurst High School, where the two districts bordered each other.

It felt good to make plans again. She refused to wonder why she was so excited over a guy she'd met once, just because a psychic had predicted the meeting. It made no sense, but neither did being run down by a car, and Cara knew that for once, she wanted something in her life to make no sense.

High clouds had covered the sky by the time Cara stood in front of Lakehurst High School. Kids were spilling out of the cream and green building, boarding buses or driving out of the parking lot. Cara felt a little nervous. This wasn't her home turf.

If Danny didn't show, Cara had one mother of a

walk home. Or she'd have to call a cab, or her mom. None of those options promised much fun.

Shivering in the sudden cool wind, Cara felt abandoned. There were hundreds of strange kids now. Then an unsettling thought struck her. Why hadn't he picked her up at Westfield? Why had he asked her to come all the way over here? And why had she *done* it? None of this sounded much like the Cara Nelson she used to know. The logical Cara would have blown off a guy like this.

"Hi."

He was standing right there, his hair blowing in the wind. Light brown hair. Red. Rust. Who cared? He wore a Lakehurst jacket and dark jeans. He looked slender, but strong. She felt her pulse galloping. "Hi," she said.

"I'm really glad you came. I wasn't sure you would."

"How come you didn't pick me up at Westfield?" she blurted out. She felt incredibly stupid the instant she'd said it.

He stared at her, then rolled his eyes upward. "That was majorly dumb, wasn't it?"

"You mean there was no reason?"

He shook his head. "No. I just—I don't know, I wrote the note and dropped the present off on my way here this morning, and— What a jerk."

Laughing, she said, "You're not kidding. I was coming up with all kinds of sinister motives."

"Like what?"

"Oh God, I don't know. Like I'd be here in a strange place and you'd have your henchmen abduct me."

94

"I don't have any henchmen." She laughed appreciatively. "Come on. I know where I want to go."

"Where?"

He stopped in the act of taking her arm. "You're *really* jumpy."

She took a breath. "Sorry. I'm very nervous about this."

"Tell me about it."

"Okay," she said. "You see, I began being nervous about an hour ago when I—"

His laughter filled her with delight. "Witty, very witty. Come on."

Oh, yes. She'd come on. What could be wrong? For starters, he had a sense of humor. She wrestled her book bag over her shoulder and said, "I really want to know where."

He was leading her across the street, weaving between school buses. "Just a few blocks away. Good place to chat."

"Or die."

He found her hand and held it. "I love paranoid women."

His car turned out to be a cute little Toyota wagon, parked on a side street. He opened the door for her and she slid in after tossing her book bag in the backseat. He got in beside her and gunned the engine. "Nice neighborhood," she said.

"It's home."

Weird, she thought as he carefully nosed into the stream of traffic. Cara sat rigidly as he drove, wishing she could put the radio on. She told herself that this was not cheating on Mark. She hadn't done anything with Danny. She was just talking to him about school newspaper stuff. Yeah. Right.

He drove through local streets to a wide cross street called Lorimer Avenue. He turned left and the road curved between old, stately trees and attractive houses. Then he pulled over, next to a forested area, marked by two ancient stone pedestals. Cara could make out the words *Sievers Beach,* carved into the pedestals.

"Come on," he said, unbuckling his seat belt.

"Uh—where are we, Danny?"

"Sievers Beach."

"Yeah, I read the sign, but I don't see a beach."

"It's down there. Back in the nineteen-twenties this was a big resort area."

"That's nice. Can't we talk in a diner or something?"

He turned to face her. "Cara, I'm going to be honest."

"Good plan."

"I want to talk seriously, and I wanted a place that was . . . a little romantic."

She glanced out the window. "This is romantic?"

"It's got all these memories. You can imagine this place years ago, with people walking down that path to the lake—"

"You mean we're at the lake?"

"Sure. About half a mile down through the woods."

"I didn't recognize any of these streets."

"Well, you live on the other side of the lake."

"Wow." She kept hearing June telling her she was going to take a ride with the redheaded boy. Okay, so she took a ride with him. But what about the darkness? What about the spiders and knives? She'd answered those questions. And it wasn't her sweet sixteen yet and she was going to live *past* her birthday and *then* take a ride with Danny.

So he wasn't going to kill her now.

Exhaling angrily, Cara unbuckled her seat belt and pushed open the car door. "Okay, but if I get a tick or something, you're toast."

She slammed the door and clenched her body against the wind, which was picking up. Danny took her hand again. "I don't want to go that deep into the woods."

"You don't?" Relief swept through her. "I am a much happier girl."

He looked at her with amusement. "This guy Mark must be a sadist."

"Mark is a bunny rabbit."

She walked with him, carefully stepping over crushed cans and other junk. A chill scuttled down her back as they passed between the gates. "This is so weird. I feel like suddenly it's going to be nineteen twenty-five or something."

"I get that feeling too," he said. "I always think about going into a parallel dimension, where my life would be different but it wouldn't affect anything here."

"I *know*," she said. "It's like I could have all these incredible adventures but meanwhile only a second would pass back here so nobody would know I was gone."

"Wait," he said. "I think this is the spot."

"This is *what* spot?" Despite the cold wind, she

was perspiring. At this point, she couldn't see the road behind them anymore.

"Hold on," he said. He pushed aside branches and seemed to be searching for something. "Yeah. Right up here. Come on."

"What am I seeing?"

"Just come on."

"I'm not going to be on a cliff or anything, am I? I can't stand heights. As you can tell by looking at me."

He smiled. "This is Long Island. There are no cliffs."

She let him take her hand and help her over a small mound of bricks and gravel. To her right a mattress lay half-rotted.

"This is what you wanted me to see? I thought you were more refined."

Laughing, he said, "No—*this* is what I wanted you to see."

He pointed. She stepped up on a boulder and stood beside him. A few feet ahead the woods stopped and Cara looked at a long grassy slope leading down to a curved beach. Cara could see the whole lake, swollen and gray. The sky seemed to race overhead.

"Wow," she said. "This is wild."

"I love this view," he said. "You can't see any houses or roads. It's like being in the wilderness."

Glancing at him, she said, "Are you sure you're not going to do anything disgusting?"

He sat down on a mossy rock. "Well I *have* done disgusting things here, when I was alone."

"Pig." She sat down next to him. "Danny, this is really beautiful. Thanks for showing it to me."

"My pleasure." It felt good to sit there, away from everything. She liked Danny. Forget prophecies. She just liked him. Not that he was the only guy she'd ever met who had intelligence, but she'd always kept guys at a distance. Face it, she was always scared to lose control. That was the beauty of Mark. She didn't like him much, so she always kept control.

"You're *deep* in thought," Danny said. "About what?"

"I'm sorry. I do that all the time."

"Daydreaming is good for your mental health."

That made her laugh. "You sound like Mr. Haller, my health teacher. Except he would yell it. *'Daydreaming* is good for your *mental health!'* "

"Sounds exciting."

"Mr. Haller's class is *not* exciting."

"Which classes *are* exciting?"

She plucked a shivering violet from the side of the rock and spun it in her hand. "My genetics class. Mr. Elkan is like a real scientist. And Mrs. Harris is a doll. She was my English honors teacher last year. She wasn't exciting, exactly, but she was so sweet."

"I had one exciting teacher," Danny said. "Mr. Hess. He was killed in a car accident. Hit and run. Never found out who did it. Happened early in the morning, while he was coming out of the deli with his roll and coffee."

"God, that's so sad."

He looked out at the lake. "He always said you can't keep planning out your life. Sooner or later, the calendar runs out. And the only thing that matters is what you did while you were here."

"*Carpe Diem,*" she intoned. "Seize the day."

"He said it was important to care about other people, and to try to make something that lasted. He really got to me."

"I can see that."

Lowering his eyes, Danny said, "As you can tell, I was never exactly a hot babe."

"You're not exactly Quasimodo," she said. "In fact, you look pretty good to me. Anyway, I'm nobody's ideal of feminine perfection."

His eyes came back up. "We waste a lot of time trying to be perfect. Mr. Hess said that too. But sooner or later, you rot and bacteria munch on you."

"This is inspiring," she said.

He smiled. "You know what I mean. When I met you at Columbia, I just *liked* you. There was a whole energy field around you. I never forgot it."

"So why didn't you say something?"

He shrugged. "I figured you wouldn't be interested in a nerd like me."

"Now *that's* a stupid comment."

"I had to grow up a little. I went out with some girls, but nothing ever happened for either of us. And this year, we exchanged school papers, Westfield and Lakehurst—"

"Right, we started doing that in September."

"And there was your name and your writing, and I kept thinking about you and finally I said, This sucks. I wanted to meet you again. That's when I came over."

Hugging herself against the wind, Cara let his words warm her. It was *everything* she'd wanted, everything. It was like she'd really, truly gone over into that other dimension. "I'm glad you did."

"Except you've got a boyfriend."

She went to him and took both of his hands. "It's not a great romance. I could break up with him, but I just met you—"

"I know," he said. "I feel weird too. I've known kids who experienced love at first sight and pretty soon it was hate at first fight."

She laughed. "I'm not sure what to do."

"I hate the rules," he said. "I'd like to just take you out on a date, like our folks used to do. And you could date Mark and then decide who you liked better."

"Yeah, right. That would go over big."

"So what happens? I really like you, Cara. I want to see you again."

She squeezed his hands more tightly. "I want to see you again too."

There was no stopping now. Her arms slid over his shoulders and he locked his hands behind the small of her back. The wind roared in her ears as she found the warmth of his mouth. He kissed sweetly, without Mark's roughness. Stunned at her own harsh breathing, she maneuvered so that she leaned hard against the tree, and drew him against her.

After an eternity, she pressed her palms against his jacket. "We have to stop," she croaked.

He eased away from her and toyed with her hair. His eyes were like wolf's eyes, but the rest of his face remained sweet. "Now I *really* like you," he said.

"I'm not usually a tease. I didn't know we'd get so caught up."

He cupped his hands around her cheeks. "Cara, I

don't want two minutes of lust at the lake. I want *you*."

"I want you too, Danny. Call me."

"I will. And I swear, next time I'll pick you up!"

That broke the spell, just in time. "Thanks for reminding me what a dork you are. Danny, you have to drive me home. I'll be grounded forever."

"Can't have that," he said. "Come on."

He held out his hand. She looked caringly at him. His hair was definitely russet. His eyes were definitely blue. She was definitely crazy about him, and she would definitely put June in her will.

CHAPTER

10

The next day Cara dragged Nancy up the hill near the tennis courts to tell her about Danny. After Nancy demanded, "What's *wrong* with you?" for the hundredth time, Cara knew she had to confide in her friend.

It was cruel to make Nancy hobble all the way up there on crutches, but Cara wanted to make sure nobody heard. Fortunately the weather had turned warm and bright. They bought hot pretzels and canned drinks in the cafeteria and Cara helped Nancy stow her crutches and stretch out leaning back against a tree.

"How's that?" Cara asked. "Okay?"

"Yes, yes, it's okay. You're driving me nuts!"

"Sorry. I just feel so bad for you."

"You *should* feel bad for me."

Cara sat cross-legged and flipped open her can of lemonade. "I know I'm being a pain," she said. "But

I feel so guilty about you getting hurt. That jerk was after *me*."

"How do you know?" Nancy asked.

"How do I know? He chased me onto somebody's front lawn!"

"But he didn't *hit* you. Maybe he was after *me*, and he just chased you to cover his tracks."

"Nancy, who would be after you?"

"Who would be after *you?*"

"It doesn't matter. June saw the car chasing people in *my* reading."

Framed against clear sky, Nancy drank her iced tea. "Boy, I never thought you'd fall for this psychic stuff."

"Neither did I. But it happened, Nancy. It really happened."

Below them, kids milled around the school. There was the smoking crowd, and a bunch of girls taking off across the football field, and a group sprawled over the steps outside the cafeteria. A couple weeks ago this was her school. She ran the newspaper; she had friends; she had Mark. Those poor jerks down there were just wandering through life, but Cara had put it all together. *Move over, jerks.*

"Cara?" Nancy prodded. "I *loved* struggling up this hill so I could watch you meditate. This is the high point of my day."

Sucking in a deep breath, Cara said, "I have something else to tell you."

"I figured."

She turned to Nancy. "You have to swear, and I mean *swear* not to say anything. I'm going crazy trying to figure out what to do."

Nancy crossed her heart. "I swear, I swear. What *is* this?"

Second deep breath. "It's about another one of June's predictions."

Nancy lowered her pretzel. "The *guy?*"

Cara nodded. "It was incredible. I was sitting in the stands and he just showed up."

"No way!"

"I'm in a big mess, Nancy."

A bank of clouds passed over the sun as Cara told Nancy about Danny's first appearance, how Danny sent her the note and how they went to Sievers Beach. The clouds passed and sunshine washed over the hill again.

Nancy was quiet for a long time. Then she bit off a chunk of pretzel and mumbled through it, "Well, you're right, Cara."

"About what?"

"You're in a big mess."

"Thanks!" Cara stood up, pushing back her unruly hair. "I don't know what to do, Nancy."

"First time I ever heard you say that."

"Well, I don't. I have such strong feelings for Danny. I've never had these feelings for a guy before. And I don't have any feelings for Mark."

"So break up with Mark and go out with Danny. What's the big deal?"

With a rueful laugh, Cara plopped back down again. "I don't know anything about Danny. Mark and I have been together for almost two years. I just can't throw that away."

"If you don't like him, what are you throwing away?"

"Security." She looked at Nancy, surprised that she was even saying this. "Mark is my boyfriend. He's taking me to the prom. He talks with my mom even when I'm not around."

"Yeah, I understand," Nancy said. She rattled the remaining iced tea in her can. "It's like you're married."

"Don't be a wench."

"No, really. You feel comfortable with him."

"That's exactly it." Cara found her can of lemonade and took a long swallow. "If I break up with Mark, that's all gone."

"You'll have Danny."

"But who *is* Danny? I don't know anything about him."

"So find out."

"Huh?"

Nancy laughed. "What's wrong with you, Cara? You're the great journalist. Find out about him. Look him up."

Cara crushed the can and tossed it into the grass. "You're right. If I like him, I like him."

"Maybe you don't *want* to find out about him, did you ever think of that? Maybe you're afraid he'll turn out to have three other girlfriends."

"Give it a rest." Of course Nancy was right. Danny was Cara's destiny. June had predicted him and Cara didn't want to know anything that would spoil the mystery.

"So what will you do?" Nancy asked.

"I don't know." Cara stood up again. "I can't keep cheating on Mark."

"That's for sure."

"This sucks." Astonished, she felt herself begin to cry. "I've never felt this way. I'm scared that someone's trying to kill me. I'm nuts about Danny. I feel like I'm in this cell and the walls are closing in."

Nancy glanced down the hill. "We can't continue this now. Bell's going to ring in two minutes."

Cara saw the kids putting out cigarettes and slowly filing back into the building. "I wanted to talk more."

"Call me when you get home."

"Definitely." She helped Nancy up, then handed over the crutches. "I need to see June again."

Nancy looked concerned. "I'm worried about you. From not believing anything, you've become obsessed."

"She *knows*," Cara said firmly. "My party's in about a week. I've got to know before then who's after me, and I've got to know about Danny. He's the one who's going to save me."

Nancy gaped at her friend. "Are you *serious* about this?"

Cara shook her head. "I don't know what I'm serious about. Come on, let's go to class."

Dyann shut the clasps of her battered violin case and returned it to its locker in the instrument room. She ached to see Eddie. Now that he was suspended for five days, she felt lost.

As she gathered her books from a chair, she heard the door swing open. Turning, she saw Mark.

"You and me have to talk," he said.

She tossed her hair. "Why?"

"Quit hassling my girlfriend."

"What are you talking about?"

He walked over to her. He was tense, his hands jammed in the pockets of his baggy jeans. "Just stay away from her."

She worked to keep her voice steady. "Look, you're the one who's doing the harassing. I just want to be left alone, so I don't know what you're talking about and I don't care."

"Don't play innocent. You tried to run her down."

Dyann felt an extraordinary sensation, like being pumped with helium. "You're nuts."

"You're the one who's nuts."

"I don't know how to tell you this, Mark. I don't have a license. I don't drive a car."

"You don't need a license," he said.

"You idiot. I don't like Cara. I like you even less. But I don't do murders, okay?"

Mark glared at her, his eyes volcanic. "I'm gonna be watching you, every minute. I'm sticking to you like skin. You understand?"

"Yes, I understand. Can I go?"

The doors opened and kids walked in. Mark stared hard at her. Then he pivoted and stalked out of the room. Dyann wondered what it would be like, once, to be with a guy like that.

The feeling left quickly, and she felt a vindictive pleasure; she'd *gotten* to him. A surge of power rippled through her. For a dreadful instant she daydreamed about actually doing it, of killing Cara.

Shifting her books in her arms, she pushed through the doors. For now, she'd have to settle for hurting Mark with the newspaper story. It almost disappointed her.

* * *

When Cara jumped off the school bus, neither car was in the driveway. In a way, Cara was glad. She needed to be by herself, without questions from Mom or Dad.

She unlocked the front door and dropped her book bag on the kitchen table. Grabbing an apple from the fruit bin, she punched the Play button on the phone answering machine, but heard only a nothing message from a friend of her mom's and a couple of blank spaces.

Depression oozed through her body. Talking with Nancy hadn't helped much. She knew what Nancy would say. What else *could* she say? Making decisions had always been Cara's speciality and now she felt helpless.

She wished Danny would knock on the door, right then. She wanted to hold him, to kiss him, to talk to him for hours. With a bitter shock of frustration, Cara realized that she'd blown off this whole issue of the *Tempest*. She knew that Dyann had handled it, and that bothered her too.

This was dumb. Angrily, she grabbed her book bag and stormed into her room. Maybe she'd start with some homework, which she hadn't done for a week. She dumped the book bag on her bed and sat down next to it. The thing was bulging with all the papers and junk she'd stuffed into it.

All right. This was Cara's comeback. Pushing back a wisp of hair, she started yanking things out of the book bag and tossing them onto the bed. After the crumpled handouts came heavy textbooks. What a mess!

Pens. She knew she had a bunch of pens in the

bottom of the bag. This was good; she'd even finish her invitation list tonight and maybe get them out in time for her party.

Holding the book bag open with her left hand, she plunged her right hand down to the bottom and rummaged around. She felt the pens rattling.

Something pinched her finger and she yanked her hand out of the bag. "Ow!" Probably one of her many lost earrings. Curious, she studied her finger and saw two tiny red punctures. Two?

Suddenly fearful, she turned the book bag over and shook it. The pens clattered out, along with some dust and candy wrappers. She held the edges of the bag apart and looked inside. Nothing there. She looked back at the pens on her bed. A yellow highlighter suddenly had a black spot on it.

No, it wasn't a black spot, it was a leg. With horror, Cara watched the spider emerge from under the pen and crawl rapidly across her bed. *"Eeeuuuu!"* she cried, and in a fury grabbed her bedspread on either side of the fleeing spider and crushed the ends together, grinding and grinding.

Breathing hard, she parted the edges of the bedspread to peek. The spider was a satisfyingly icky mess. It was a tiny thing, not exactly a tarantula, but pretty disgusting anyway.

Cara got up and went to her desk for a tissue. She stumbled, and a knifelike pain stabbed her finger. She cried out and swiftly stared at her hand. Nothing there. Scared now, she grabbed tissues and started back for the bed.

Another surge of pain made her seize her wrist. Perspiring, she tried to stay calm. That stupid spider must have really bitten her hard. She sat down on her bed again and scraped the remains of the spider into the tissue. She stared at the black stuff.

Black widow?

A third assault of pain made her drop the tissue. She'd never felt pain like this. Her legs felt like ginger ale and she started to hyperventilate. *Call the police,* she ordered herself. *Quick.*

She stood up, and this time the pain came in waves. Lunging for her desk, she grabbed her chair desperately, and pulled it over as she fell. She rolled back and forth on her rug, squeezing her arm so tightly it turned white. She heard her screams as if they came from somewhere else. The pain was spreading now, stabbing up her arm into her shoulder.

She turned over on her stomach and crawled toward her desk. The pain forced her to stop. She wasn't going to make it. This was so stupid—her phone was right there, right on her desk, and she couldn't get to it. Horrified, she felt her throat swell and when she tried to speak, only gagging sounds came out.

A torrent of pain doubled her up. She was going to die. She couldn't breathe at all. Deep in her throat, she sobbed, "Mommy—" as sheets of flame passed in front of her eyes.

CHAPTER

11

I'm so tired, Cara thought. Whatever they'd given her packed a knockout punch. Lazily, she held up her hand. Her bitten finger was bandaged and her hand and wrist were puffy.

When she hoisted herself to a sitting position, she could see the nurse's station. Not too busy today, except for the spider victim. She hugged herself as her stomach cramped. A nurse appeared and eased her back down. "Take it slow, honey. You're still a little cooked."

"Am I going to live?" She knew it was a dumb question.

"Yes. But now you know you're allergic to insect bites."

"Some allergy. Where's my mom and dad?"

"They went out to get coffee."

"Do they know I'm alive?"

She heard the nurse chuckle. "I think so."

Sleep blanketed her again. Then, suddenly awake, she sat up and shivered in the cold. Her eyes swept the walls, finally locating a clock. Eight-thirty. *Eight-thirty?* Sinking back against the pillow, she felt stunned. Six hours. She remembered trying to reach the phone and she remembered how much it hurt, but that was it.

Mom's voice alerted her and she looked over toward the nurse's station. Mom still wore her white uniform from the school cafeteria. Cara felt guilty; they hadn't even changed their clothes.

She waved as they came over. They looked half-dead. For a second Cara didn't want them here. Then Mom was hugging her and she hugged back. Dad bent down to give her a clumsy kiss.

They stood over her, peering down. "I feel like a newborn," she said, "with you guys staring at me."

"Newborn is a good word," Mom said. "We thought you were gone."

"Geez," Dad said, "I keep thinking of all the times you played outside, with all the bugs and spiders around. Who knew?"

"Well, I got that tick bite once."

"But you didn't blow up like a balloon."

"I blew up? Really?"

Mom said, "Don't sound so excited. I was never so scared in my life."

"Did you guys find me?"

"I found you," Mom said. "I walked into the house and heard these sounds like an animal dying. Then I saw you on the floor, with the phone in your hand . . ."

She turned away. As Dad rubbed her neck, Cara said, "So I did get the phone. I didn't remember."

"Yeah," Dad said, "but you weren't calling anybody."

"What did you do?" Cara asked Mom.

"I called nine-one-one and gave you CPR, what do you think?"

"You *did?* That is so outrageous!"

"What did you think I would do, watch you die?"

"No, but most moms couldn't do that."

"Well, I did take the course down at the church."

Cara leaned back, feeling tired again. "Did I ride in an ambulance?"

"Yes, you did," Mom said. "Me too."

"I can't remember."

"You were slightly unconscious."

"I *hate* that I missed it," Cara pouted. "It must have been wild, racing through red lights. I've always wanted to do that."

Mom sighed. "Well, you can ride with me when I have my stroke."

A pudgy doctor came over. Smiling, he said, "How is she doing?"

"She's fine," Mom said.

The doctor smiled more broadly. "I'm Dr. Kim. How are you feeling, Cara?"

"Pretty weak."

He leaned over and lifted her eyelids with his thumb. Setting his clipboard at the foot of the bed, he said, "I'm going to manipulate your abdomen and your legs. It won't hurt."

Amused, Cara saw her dad turn away. She looked at the fluorescent ceiling lights as Dr. Kim pressed down on her stomach. It hurt a little. Then he was twirling her legs between his hands.

He picked up his clipboard again. "The abdomen is soft, and the legs are loose," he said. "So things look good."

Cara watched him write. "Doctor, it was a spider. In my book bag."

He smiled at her. "I know. Your mother found the dead spider in a tissue and brought it in."

"Was it a black widow?" Cara asked.

"Yes, it was," Dr. Kim said. "Usually, the reaction wouldn't be so severe, but you appear to be allergic."

"How did you save me?"

Dad said, "Don't be so dramatic."

Dr. Kim said, "The EMTs gave you a big dose of serum, and we followed up with antihistamines. We also used ice to bring down the swelling. You'll feel stiff for a while, but you'll be fine." He turned to Mom and Dad. "She should carry an insect bite kit with her. If she were stung by a swarm of bees or wasps, the results could be fatal."

"I'm never going outside again," Cara said.

"It's unlikely to happen," Dr. Kim said. "But the insect bite kit will protect you in an emergency." He tucked his pen back into his white smock. "What was a black widow spider doing in your book bag?"

"*I* didn't put it there," Cara said.

"I'm sure not. But that's why you were bitten. The black widow is usually very shy, but when you felt around in the bottom of the bag she felt threatened and attacked."

"Don't look at *me*," Mom said. "I can't imagine where her book bag has been."

Dr. Kim laughed softly and left. Dad said, "They told me we could take her home as soon as she feels okay."

"I feel okay," Cara said.

"Supergirl," Mom commented. "Considering what you looked like a couple of hours ago, I think you should rest for a while."

"But you've been here for six hours!" Cara said. "And I'm hungry."

Dad looked really uncomfortable standing for so long. "Where *was* your book bag?" he asked.

"All over the place," she said. "I was talking with Nancy near the tennis courts at school, and I put it on the ground when I wait for the bus. Who knows when the spider got in there?"

"Well, be a little more careful," Mom said.

Tell them, her brain screamed. That spider hadn't gotten into her bag on the hill. It was an open area with a couple of trees and no spider webs. And there were no black widows on the sidewalk where she waited for the bus. Even the day before when she'd gone into the woods with Danny, she'd left her book bag in his car.

"Cara?" Dad said. "Are you okay?"

She forced a smile. "I was just thinking about stuff."

"What stuff?" Mom asked.

Mom knew something was wrong. She was the best psychic around. "Nothing," she said.

Mom perched on the edge of the bed and smoothed back Cara's hair. "Baby, why don't you talk to us?"

She felt her heart thudding. "There's nothing to talk about. It's just that first some guy chases me in a car and now there's a black widow spider in my book bag. I think someone is trying to get me."

Now she was crying. Dad looked lost. "What the hell is that supposed to mean? Who are you talking about?"

Mom said, "Jack, let her calm down."

"I want to know what's going on here."

Squeezing Cara's hand, Mom said, "Can you be a little more specific? Is there a name you can give us?"

She shook her head. "No. I can't imagine who it is."

"Is there someone angry at you? A student? A teacher?"

"No. Dyann Wilson doesn't like me a lot but she's not exactly the killer type."

"Are you sure?"

"Yeah, I'm sure. She can't even drive a car. And I don't think she'd ever touch a black widow spider."

Dad sighed impatiently. "Well, I'd like a straight story. If some creep is going after my kid, I'm going after him. But I need to have a name."

Cara forced herself to breathe deeply. "Daddy, I can't give you a name."

"Maybe someone is just trying to scare you," Mom suggested.

"Well, it's a pretty sick person!" Cara said. "I mean, he almost killed Nancy, and that spider could have bit *anyone* who reached into the bag. I never hurt anyone enough to hate me so much."

"Okay, sweetie," Mom said. "You'll take a day off from school tomorrow."

"No!"

"It's not negotiable."

Sighing, Cara said, "Okay."

After a pause, Mom said, "Do you want to cancel your sweet sixteen party?"

"No way!"

"Okay, okay, I thought I'd ask. You're in pretty bad shape and it wouldn't be much fun if you were scared to death."

Cara realized her hands were clenched into fists. "I'm having my party. This asshole isn't going to ruin my life."

Mom stood up. "Okay, let's go sign her out. We'll stop for something to eat and then get her to bed."

Mom and Dad went over to the desk. Cara gazed down at her hands. Her body felt like the whole football team had kicked it around. Why couldn't she tell them the truth? Mom had saved her life. Mom and Dad cared about her more than anyone in the world. But Mom and Dad would be so disappointed that she had gone to a psychic, and then they'd get June's name and have her arrested and Thea would be dragged into it, and Nick and Nancy and Dyann. God, it would be so awful.

Danny. She needed him now. Never, in her whole life, had she felt so alone and so helpless.

Dyann still wore the short flowered dress she'd worn to school, as she hurried down the path from her house. Her throat pulsed with tension; it was getting harder and harder to come up with excuses for leaving the house.

Anxious, Dyann arrived at the main road and saw Eddie's car. She depended so much on its being there. She ran across the road and swiftly slid into the front seat. She liked the musty smell now, felt comforted by it.

"Hi," she said.

"You look pretty that way."

"Thanks. I wore it for you."

"How was Cara today?"

She felt the gall come up in her throat. "Cara was the freaking main event, what do you think? Little Miss Muffett, bitten by the spider. God, she was like a war hero."

"Pisses you off."

"Yes, it pisses me off." She slumped down in the seat. "Why do you play with my head? You know what I'm feeling. It was supposed to feel good, taking the newspaper away." She turned to him. "She was back there today, dictating to everybody. What was the use, Eddie? I kick her and she bounces back. It doesn't change anything for me."

"Do you hate her?"

"Yes!"

"Wow. Strong."

"Do you have a drink?"

"Here."

She took the bottle from him and let the burning sweetness ease her fever.

"When's your issue come out?"

"In a day or two."

"Then it's your turn."

"For what? The jocks will get steamed and make my life hell again."

"They'll be afraid of you."

"No, they won't."

"Yes, they will. You cut them, and they were all over you. Now you cut them deeper. And they know you'll cut them again."

"How? Cara's got the newspaper back."

"She's more scared than the jocks."

"She doesn't act it."

"She knows someone's after her. You know how that feels? It takes you apart, piece by piece."

The alcohol buzzed in her head. "It's just luck that June predicted someone would go after her and these things are happening. It doesn't mean anything else will happen."

His hand was suddenly stroking her hair. "It's not luck," he said.

"What isn't?"

"You know what I mean."

The realization punched an icy hole in her stomach. "Eddie, don't tell me this."

"How much do you want things to happen?"

She couldn't see anything but the glint of his sunglasses. "Eddie, come on. Tell me you didn't do this stuff."

"I didn't say I did anything."

She faced forward again and gulped from the bottle. "Don't do that to me."

He laughed. "Cara's on the edge. What would you like to happen to her?"

"I'd like her to die. I'd like to see her face when she knew it was over and tell her 'Too bad, babe, you can't control everything. Sometimes it just sucks.' "

He took the bottle again. "How far will you go?"

"What does that mean? Will I take a knife and kill her? I can't do it."

"What if it got done?"

"Meaning what?"

"Would that help you?"

"Oh, man, Eddie, every time I listen to you, I feel good, and then it all falls apart again. I hate them so much, Eddie. Do you know how many times I've looked at Mom's razor and come *this close?*"

"So you've been on the edge?"

"Yes."

He stroked her hair again. "You're close to good stuff. It's how far you'll go."

She turned to him, eyes filling. "All right, Eddie, how far do you want me to go? Stop screwing around and tell me how to do this."

"Want me to?"

"Yes, I want you to."

Something glittered in the darkness of the car. He held it up and the streetlight defined it. As she stared at the knife blade, he said, "Want me to?"

Her vision blurred and she saw kaleidoscopes of silver shapes as he turned the knife. Her stomach heaved. "Yes," she said.

He curled a hand around the back of her neck. She could barely breathe as he kissed her. She felt the flat of the knife blade touch her cheek and it sent electric shocks through her.

"Yes?" he said.

"*Yes.*"

She vaguely heard the *whoosh* of cars going by as he enfolded her, the sleeves of his trench coat like dark wings.

CHAPTER

12

Cara's hand hovered over the telephone in the English office. This wasn't like her. She'd never been scared to make a phone call.

Well, that was then, this was now. She'd never been chased by a killer car or bitten by a black widow.

Angry, Cara punched in the number of Lakehurst High School. If her chest pounded any harder, there'd be earthquake reports.

"Lakehurst High School, good morning."

"Hi, I need to get in touch with Danny Schonberg. He's a senior there."

"Who's calling, please?"

"This is his older sister." Quickly she added, "Nothing's wrong—don't scare him!"

"Just a moment."

Incredible how she was shaking. Nancy was such a witch for suggesting this. Cara raised her index finger from the receiver and stared at the tiny pink dots from the spider bite. Her stomach reeled.

From the hallway she could hear the homeroom announcements over the PA. Only the Mighty Mite could get herself excused from homeroom to make a phone call *on a department chairperson's phone!* That brought a flickering smile.

The new *Tempest* was being distributed in homeroom that morning. Cara felt a sharp pang as she imagined kids reading it. This one was not hers, it was Dyann's.

"Excuse me, Miss . . . Schonberg?"

The voice startled Cara. "Uh . . . yeah?"

"I'm sorry, we have no student by that name. Are you sure you wanted this school?"

Her head throbbed. "Yes. Lakehurst High School. On Grand Avenue?"

"That's us, but we have no student named Daniel Schonberg on our rolls."

"But he *has* to be there. He's on the school paper. Are you sure you looked for the right spelling?"

"I checked all possible spellings, miss. I'm really sorry."

Cara felt her face grow hot. "Okay. I don't know what the problem is. Thanks anyway."

"You're very welcome."

Long after the click, Cara held the phone. The looming metal bookshelves seemed to slant in toward her. She wasn't totally surprised; something had told her Danny didn't go to that school. And there was no way she'd met him at Columbia. She would have remembered.

No friends. As she hung up the phone, she realized

that when he had met her at Lakehurst, not one person said hello to him. If he were editor of the school newspaper, he'd know *somebody*. And his car was parked way over on a side street, not in the student parking lot.

So why did he make her go there? If he'd picked her up at Westfield, she'd never have seen that he didn't know anybody. Why would he *want* to make her suspicious?

Why did he lie in the first place?

Cara perched on a table. About two minutes until the bell, and she had to get to social issues. She couldn't even call Danny because she didn't have his phone number. What hurt the most was how much she needed him.

There went the bell. Infuriated, Cara jumped off the table and grabbed her book bag, which was a shade lighter and a lot smaller since her Mom had put it through the washing machine. *I can't do this,* she despaired.

A loud bang made her turn. Mark stood at the doorway. "You gave me a heart attack! What's the matter?"

His expression was wild under his maroon cap. He held a newspaper, like a rolled-up club, in his fist. "You know what's the matter."

"No, I don't, Mark."

"How could you do this?"

"What?"

"Want me to spell it for you?"

"Mark, I've got to go to class."

She slung her book bag over her shoulder and tried

to squeeze past him. He threw an arm across her path. "Get back there," he said.

"Cut it out, Mark."

"Get *back!*" He shoved her and her breath stopped. Tripping over the wastebasket, she thumped against the desk.

"You're crazy."

"No, you're crazy." He brandished the newspaper. "You're going to be killed, babe. Don't bother going anywhere because if I don't rip your heart out, some other guy will."

"Mark, if you're talking about a story in the *Tempest—*"

"Don't jerk me around!" he screamed.

She slid past him and backed away, standing near the bookcases. He pivoted to face her again as the doorway darkened. Two teachers were coming in, Mrs. Oslansky and Ms. Durand. As they entered, they acknowledged Cara and Mark.

"Hello," Mrs. Oslansky said.

"Anything we can do for you folks?" Ms. Durand asked.

Cara could smell their perfume. "No," she said tightly. "I was just going to class."

Mrs. Oslansky turned to Mark. "Are you here to pick up books?"

"No. I'm going."

Cara almost enjoyed his discomfort, but right then she just wanted to get out of there and go somewhere to think. She stepped into the hallway, which was less crowded now. Never would she make her class on time.

Then Mark was there, tugging at her wrist. She spun to face him. "Get out of my face, Mark. I'll scream. I swear to God."

"Come outside with me."

Cara knew it was no big deal to cut out of social issues. Mrs. Canterbury would probably just bring in doughnuts anyway, as she usually did, and talk about her son in the army.

"All right," she said.

"This way." He indicated the double metal doors right behind them. Releasing her wrist, he gave her a slight shove. She glared at him and they went outside.

Sunlight blinded her and heat pressed down. They said on the radio that morning it would be near eighty. "Man, it's brutal out," she said.

"Keep going."

She wrenched herself away from him and dumped her book bag on a wooden picnic table just outside the cafeteria. Along the chain link fence behind her, kids hung out and smoked. She felt that everyone was watching.

He confronted her, still gripping the newspaper. "Okay," he said, "let's have it out."

"I swear to God, Mark, I don't know what you're talking about."

He shook the newspaper at her. "It's your paper, right?"

"You're talking about *this* issue of the *Tempest*?"

"Good answer."

She exhaled. "I didn't work on this issue. I've been out of commission, remember? Spider bite? Nearly dead?"

"You were out of school for a day," he snapped. "Don't try to bull me."

"No bull, Mark. I didn't write any of this issue. Zero. Zip. *Comprende?*"

"You're telling me you didn't know about the sports article?"

"That's what I'm telling you, jerk."

He exhaled sharply, probably trying to decide whether to believe her. She couldn't take the heat or the brightness of the sun. The late bell sounded inside the building.

"Who did the issue?"

She almost said, "Dyann," but stopped herself. He'd just find her and attack her. Not that Cara would mind, but she didn't want it on her hands. "The whole staff, I guess. I wasn't around. Can I look at it?"

Still confused, he handed over the paper. She opened it to the back page. First she noticed that the layout was sharper than usual, with big headlines and photos. A wave of jealousy passed over her. Then she read the lead story, under the headline, Westfield Sports Don't Hack It. " 'Spring traditionally brings hope for rebirth and growth, but for the Westfield baseball and lacrosse teams, it brings despair. Our boys have lost games, skills, and motivation—' "

"Keep going," Mark said. "Read the whole thing. You know what's going to happen when college coaches read this? No chance for a scholarship. Down the tubes."

She scanned the rest of the article, which was deadly. There were graphs and everything. It was done right too. Quotes from coaches and players, comparisons with former teams. Westfield athletes were more interested in parties than practice, the article accused. They showed no commitment, no spirit. The indictment was total.

As she read, Cara felt some of Mark's fury. The byline was Nick's, but this was Dyann's revenge. The jocks could throw fits if they wanted, but nothing in here was untrue, and everyone would know it. She'd blindsided them.

"Wow," she said, lowering the paper. "Pretty savage."

"Yeah, no kidding." His voice nearly cracked. "I'm dead, Cara. You know what I'm talking about?"

"I don't think they'll take away your scholarships, Mark. College coaches don't read high school papers, do they?"

"Yeah, they do. They look for stats, for players to watch. Now they'll know which players to cut."

"It may not be that bad. Have your coach write letters. Rebut the story."

"It's too late for that. By the next issue of the *Tempest,* it'll all be over. This really sucks. You're telling me Brill okayed this?"

Cara wondered herself. "I don't know. I told you, I wasn't involved."

"How come I don't buy that?"

Her fear and confusion coalesced into cold anger. "I don't know, Mark. How come you don't buy that? Why do you think I'd do this to you?"

"Because you're sore at me for hassling Dyann."

"No way! You think I'd do *this* to you?"

"I didn't know what else to think."

"Maybe you didn't think at all."

He tugged at his cap bill. "Okay, okay. Now I know you didn't do it. No problem."

"Really sincere apology."

"All right. I'm *sorry*, okay?"

"No, it's not okay!" She hugged herself to stop her shaking. "None of this is okay. Everything made sense a couple of weeks ago, and now nothing makes sense. Someone's trying to kill me, and nobody's taking it seriously."

He studied her, hands in his pockets. "Okay, I was wrong about that too. I should have paid more attention to you."

Shaking her head, she said, "You don't get it. I'm not talking about attention."

She could *feel* his eyes narrow. "So what is this all leading to? Are you dumping me? Is that what you're saying?"

Yes, it was what she was saying, and she couldn't believe it. Her words had their own life. Maybe it was the sun frying her brains. She was ditching him for a guy who lied to her. Mark had *never* lied to her. Or loved her.

"Mark, I just need time to think," she said.

"Bull. Who's the other guy?"

"Don't accuse me, Mark!"

He stood right over her, his shadow cold against the sun. "Don't play me for a fool. I want to know who he is."

"He's nobody," she said. "He doesn't exist. Can't you just accept what I'm saying without your stupid ego getting into it?"

"Not that easy," he said. "You don't just walk out on me."

"Come on, Mark. This isn't a game. My life is falling apart. I don't hate you, but right now I just can't handle the relationship. I want a little time."

"No way," he said. "If you walk, you're out of my life. I don't give second chances."

She lowered her head so he wouldn't see her crying. "Your head is so thick."

"You're not kidding my head is thick. My head was thick for ever going out with you. What do you think you are, Cara? You're no model. You think a million guys are going to knock themselves out over some skinny little witch? I was your best shot, babe. I took plenty of heat for being with you. Everyone told me I could do better. Except I was loyal, but that's something you don't know about. Don't come looking for me again." He walked away, cursing her.

A girl with platinum hair stood over Cara. "Are you okay?"

"Yeah, fine."

"You sure?"

Cara nodded, embarrassed. The girl shrugged and walked away. Cara looked up, breathing hard. She'd find Danny and love him, no matter what school he went to. And maybe she'd quit the paper too.

Feeling like wet wash, Cara stood up and hoisted her book bag. She knew she was feeling sorry for herself, but she did it anyway. Things would be tough enough when Mom found out that she'd broken up with Mark *and* cut class. She trudged back to the building.

CHAPTER
13

By sixth period Cara's breakup with Mark was Headline News. She'd gone through a box of tissues and every teacher had yelled at her for daydreaming.

Seventh period was lunch and she had to get away. She shoved her book bag into her locker and pedaled out the front doors. Nancy would be waiting in the cafeteria, but no way could Cara go there.

Frustration bubbled in her throat as she crossed the parking lot. So where did she go now? She could walk to the deli or hike to the ecology pond. Reality: There was *nowhere* to go. She'd never run from her life before.

She began to walk, dragging her fingertips along the fence. "Skinny little witch" kept echoing in her brain. *He was just being a moron,* she reassured herself. Yeah, but he was right. She'd known the truth from seventh grade on, but she made up for it with loudness, cheerfulness, and efficiency.

When she had covered the baseball team the year before last, Mark thought she was a riot. Then he got hurt and they sat in the stands together and talked. He asked her to hang with his group and then go to a party. It was one of those open house horrors, with two kegs and a bouncer, and the cops breaking it up. Her mom had thought Cara was at Nancy's house. Well, parents shouldn't know everything.

She'd made out with Mark at the party. That was the start of the romance, which chugged along really great for months. He was so comfortable, so predictable. She controlled him. She controlled her heart.

Her throat clenched and she choked back tears. It hurt more than she expected. Maybe she could call him up, talk it over. This wasn't really a breakup, just a fight.

A steady humming noise intruded on her jangled thoughts, and Cara realized she'd been hearing it for a while. Turning to her right, she saw the beige Toyota and Danny's elbow resting in the open window. Her stomach flip-flopped.

"Are you okay?" he said. "I've been calling your name out for three blocks."

Instinctively, her hand flew to her hair to straighten it. "I'm sorry."

"I came to take you to lunch."

"How did you know I had lunch this period?"

"I checked your schedule in the office."

She reddened and thought, *Well, I'm not the only one who investigates.* "I don't have much time."

"You have a lifetime," he said.

"Okay."

She ran around the car and slid in, slamming the

door. He took off with a roar, then slowed for a red light. "What's up?" he asked. His hair blew in the wind (red; definitely, absolutely red). His stylish shirt was half-unbuttoned, giving him a romantic look. He shielded his eyes as he watched the light.

"Don't you have sunglasses?" she asked.

"I keep losing them."

The light changed and he charged forward. She sat half twisted in the seat so she could keep looking at him. "You really know when to show up," she said.

"Well, I could see you were pretty tense."

"Yeah, you could say that."

"What happened?"

"I broke up with Mark."

His hand tightened on the steering wheel. "Not because of what we talked about?"

"Why, wouldn't that be a good reason?"

"I don't know." He glanced at her, then back at the road. "I feel too responsible."

Impulsively, she slid next to him and toyed with the hair at the back of his neck. "Danny, I'm falling apart. I need to be put back together."

"Get some Krazy Glue."

"Don't make a joke out of it!"

"You have a temper."

She let go of him and sat back, angry. "I'm sorry. It's been a disgusting day."

The road wound around the lake, then past shopping centers and a bank with a big electric temperature sign. Eighty-two degrees—at the beginning of April. A week ago it had been forty-five.

"Crazy weather," she said.

"April is schizoid," he said. "Can't decide if it's winter or summer."

"I like that." She liked everything he said. Cara shut her eyes to the bump and flow of the car. Never would they make it back in time for her eighth period class. Two cuts in one day. Who cared?

He slowed and she opened her eyes. They were pulling off the road. To the right, beyond a green chain link fence, was a small park. "Stopping?" she said.

"Let's go on the swings."

She grabbed his hand as they entered the park, then yanked loose and began to run. By the time she reached the playground, her throat was burning and she was gasping for breath. Laughing, she turned to watch him approach.

"Old man!" she taunted.

He smiled as he reached her. "Let's see how good you are where it counts."

"Huh?"

He pointed to the swings. "How far are you willing to go?"

"Farther than you!"

She raced for the swings and hoisted herself into one. Laughing, she watched Danny's legs drag in the sand. She flexed her knees and pumped hard. Her stomach tickled with fright.

"Higher!" she shouted. The chains jerked and thumped, and the swing set began to rock on its base. The rattle and jingle delighted her.

"Higher!" she tried to yell, but couldn't get enough breath. Then the chain became taut, twisting the swing in midair. She shrieked and let the swing slow.

She sat for a moment, gasping, then noticed Danny. His face was flushed too. They both broke into laughter at the same time.

"Seesaw!" she cried and catapulted from the swing to race him. No contest. He reached the seesaw first and straddled one end, keeping the board level.

She climbed aboard, and Danny sat down hard. Her end shot up and she yelped, gripping the handle hard and lifting her legs onto the board. She looked down at him and said, "Come on, you creep! Let me down!"

"Never," he said. "I've got you where I want you."

"Danny, come on!"

"Do you love me?"

"Yes!"

He stood up suddenly, and she came down with a mighty thump. With a savage curse, Cara stood up and rubbed her rear end. "You pig. That was pretty juvenile."

"No," he said. "You're a pretty juvenile."

She pulled him down with her. Lying in moist grass, she shut her eyes and moved her head under his, until the kisses ran liquidly into each other. Her hands moved tenderly across his back and up into his hair.

A sliver of upbringing reminded her that this was a public park in the middle of the day. She gently pushed him off and lay under the hot sun, breathing raggedly. He plucked a blade of grass and tickled her nose and cheek with it.

"Danny?" she said.

"Yeah?"

136

"Why did you lie?"

"About what?"

"About going to Lakehurst High School."

His eyes studied her. "You checked?"

"Yes. I didn't know anything about you."

A smile lifted his lips. "I knew you were a reporter at heart."

"Why did you lie?"

"I'm out of high school," he said. "I went to college for a year, and then dropped out. I'm drifting now. I work different jobs."

"So what's wrong with that?"

He shrugged. "I didn't want to scare you off. I figured if you thought I was a senior on the school paper I'd be familiar territory. I wanted a chance with you."

"How did you even know about me? It wasn't at Columbia."

"Yes, it was."

"I don't remember you!"

"That's where I went to college. I worked on the paper there and figured I'd check out the high school stuff. The rest was pretty much as I told you, except I made up all the Lakehurst stuff to meet you. Was I a fool?"

She pulled his head down and kissed him. Then she said, "Yes, you were a fool. Who cares if you're seventeen or nineteen? Is that what you are, nineteen?"

"Twenty," he said.

Mom's face hovered in her mind, horrified. "So, twenty. I'll be sixteen soon." The thought jolted her. "Danny. I want you to come to my sweet sixteen.

Oh God, I know what that must sound like. A bunch of ditzy teenage girls with too much makeup. I'll understand if you don't want to go near it, but I want you there. You're my new boyfriend. Aren't you?"

"Did you fill out an application?"

"Shut up." She grabbed him around his neck and shut her eyes again.

When they walked back to the car, Cara's head spun like a runaway carousel. But as she gripped Danny's hand, part of her felt ashamed and frightened. This was too fast. Her mom and dad would freak. Twenty. College dropout. And what if he was lying about that?

But Danny was supposed to be here. Danny was meant to save her.

She sat in the Toyota, staring out the window, as he made a U-turn and drove back toward the school. "Danny Schonberg," she murmured.

"You rang?"

"It's a nice name. What does it mean?"

"Schonberg? It means beautiful mountain."

She laughed and glanced at him. "That's you. A beautiful mountain."

"Don't make fun of my physique. I work hard to get it like this."

Panicky, she said, "I wasn't making fun!" She touched his shoulder. "Don't be mad."

"I couldn't be mad at you, babe. Not when I'm coming to your sweet sixteen."

The lake glittered in the sun as they passed it. "Danny, I love you."

"I love you too, Cara."

She let the sound of the words caress her. Mark

had never said them. Maybe once or twice, when she'd bullied him. Never like Danny had said them. What was she going to tell her mom and dad?

Suddenly she wanted to see June again. She didn't want to die, and she didn't want to lose Danny. June could read him. And if Cara brought something of his, a psychic was supposed to be able to tell a lot from it. God, she couldn't believe she was so conniving.

She glanced at him, desperately searching his body. Watch? Belt? Wallet? *Just ask for his underwear.*

They were near the school. Cara sneaked her hand toward the glove compartment. The door flipped down.

He glanced at her. "What was that?"

"Your glove compartment attacked me." Her voice sounded as if she'd sucked helium.

"Yeah, it does that."

Breathing hard, she looked down. Papers, a pencil—whoops, what was that? An earpiece? She reached in and slid out a pair of sunglasses. Heart thudding, she glanced at him. He was focused straight ahead. Her hand closed over the sunglasses and glided back to her thigh. With her free hand, she shut the glove compartment door. Sweat ran down her back.

"Home," he said, pulling up to the gate. The buses were already lined up in front of the school, red lights flashing. The last bell would ring in a few minutes.

All at once Cara felt embarrassed about being seen with him. "I am going to be in such trouble," she said. "I've cut more classes today than in my whole life."

"We never had lunch."

"It's okay. I had you instead."

She arched toward him, slipping the sunglasses into her pocket. "See you soon."

"How about a real date?" he asked. "Like coming to your house with flowers and taking you to a movie? I mean, instead of just riding around."

"I'd like that," she said. "I really would."

He said, "I'm sorry about the breakup with Mark."

"Don't sweat it," she said. "I've got to go."

"Glad I found you."

"Me too." She kissed him once more, then fumbled for the door handle and got out. She watched him pull away and let her right hand slip into her pocket and feel the sunglasses. This had to be the most insane day of her life.

CHAPTER

14

Cara paced back and forth in Nancy's room, a cordless phone at her ear. Nancy lay on her bed. As Cara waited for someone to pick up, she watched Nancy lean forward and rub her cast.

"Does it hurt?" she asked.

"It *itches*," Nancy complained.

Click. The ringing stopped. "This is Dr. Brady's office. I'm not in now, but if you care to leave a message . . ."

Ferociously, Cara pushed the hangup button. "Answering machine."

"Well, it is kind of late," Nancy reminded her.

"I always get the machine. Late. Early. Whatever." She flipped the phone onto Nancy's desk and sat in her chair. "She just doesn't want to talk to me."

"Why not?"

"Because she doesn't want to tell me what's going

to happen." Drumming her fingertips on the desk, Cara tried to think. "I told you about last time. She doesn't want to get sued for predicting my death."

Nancy's crutches leaned against her bed, making Cara remember. She glanced again at the window, which was black now. "Call me when you're ready to leave Nancy's house," Mom had said. "I know Mrs. Chu doesn't have a car, so I'll come get you."

"You're pretty deep in thought," Nancy said.

"I was thinking about how dumb my life is," Cara replied. "How I can't even walk home from your house, which is around the corner."

"Better safe than sorry," Nancy said.

"It's so *stupid*." On her feet again, Cara went to the window. Through the black tangle of trees in Nancy's backyard, Cara could see the lights of houses. Now and then, a flash of headlights flickered among the branches. Cara shuddered.

"You're so sad tonight," Nancy said.

"Tell me about it."

"Okay," Nancy said. "It all started when you were a little girl . . ."

Laughing, Cara turned from the window. "Very cute." She flopped onto the bed and gazed dolefully at Nancy. "I've *got* to see June. My party is in a week."

"Oh, yeah—I got your invitation."

"You did? Let me see."

"It's on my desk, under all that junk."

Cara bounded off the bed and sifted through the papers on Nancy's desk. She picked up the brightly colored invitation and scanned it.

Flipping the invitation back onto the desk, Cara said, "Don't forget to RSVP."

"I'm telling you yes now."

"No good. I want an official phone call."

"No way."

Cara lunged for the bed and seized the pillow. Nancy hung on to it, squealing. The girls wrestled for possession of the pillow, twisting and yanking, laughing wildly. Cara finally jerked it free and swung it down on Nancy's head. Nancy brought up her arms to protect herself, screaming, "No! I'm injured! No fair!"

Gasping, Cara dropped the pillow and said, "I've got to see her, Nancy!"

Nancy's face was flushed, her hair madly tousled. "You just want to find out about Danny. You couldn't care less about your stupid death."

"I want to find out about Danny *and* my death."

Downstairs, the phone rang. For an instant, Cara thought *Danny* and then realized she wasn't in her own house. From her purse, she fished out the sunglasses she'd found in Danny's glove compartment. "Danny told me he lost his sunglasses. But they were right there."

"Oh, come on," Nancy chided. "Everyone loses *everything* in the glove compartment."

"Okay, so he forgot they were there. Anyway, June can use them."

Nancy shook her head. "I can't believe this is you."

"Well, I've changed." She gripped the sunglasses and rhythmically punched the side of the bureau. Then she said, "Thea would know her home number."

"Thea's not going to tell you."

"It's worth asking." Cara picked up the portable phone. "You know, I haven't seen Dyann for days now and it feels wonderful."

"Are you going back to the *Tempest?*" Nancy asked.

"I don't know. What's Thea's number?"

"How should I know what her number is? Look it up."

"Where's the phone book?"

"Downstairs in the kitchen."

Cara slammed the phone down. "Terrific."

"*Sorry,*" Nancy said. "I don't usually keep the phone book in my room!"

"All right, all right." Cara stomped out of the room and down the stairs. In the bright kitchen, Cara riffled through the phone book, nearly forgetting Thea's last name for a minute. She found the number and whispered it five times to memorize it.

As she started back upstairs, Mrs. Chu called from the den, "Cara, your mother was on the phone before. She said you should come home as soon as possible—no emergency but it's important."

"She said to come home?" Cara said.

"Yes, she did."

"Not that she'd pick me up?"

"Those were her words, Cara."

"Wow," Cara mused. "She *trusts* me. Thanks, Mrs. C."

"You're welcome."

Nancy was sitting up, her legs dangling over the bed. Cara asked, "Where are *you* going?"

"Nowhere. My butt starts to burn when I lie there too long."

Cara scooped up the phone and punched in the number. *Pick up*, she intoned. One ring, two rings, then a click. "Hello?"

"Thea! It's Cara Nelson."

"Oh. Hi."

"Listen, Thea. Your aunt June called me and left a message on my machine, but the dumb thing's on the fritz and the phone number's all garbled. Do you have it?"

"Aunt June called you?"

Nancy was staring at Cara with her mouth open. Cara stifled a giggle. "Yeah, sometime this afternoon, I guess. We just got home from shopping and there was the message."

"She wouldn't be in her office now," Thea said.

"I *know*," Cara agreed. "But I think this was her home number because she says something about being at home until nine. Anyway, do you have it? I'm really worried about why she called."

"Okay, just a minute."

Cara pumped her fist in the air. Nancy stared at Cara in wonderment. Thea came back on the phone and Cara repeated the number as Thea said it. "Thanks a zillion," she added.

"I hope you got the message right," Thea said. "Aunt June will kill me."

"She won't kill you, don't worry." Cara pressed the hangup button and let out the laughter that had built up in her. "She is so *stupid!* I can't believe it!"

"I can't believe you *did* that," Nancy said. "Thea's going to get punished forever."

"I'll get her off the hook, don't worry." Anxiously, Cara pressed the numbers. "Anyway, Aunt June probably knows about this already."

The phone was ringing. Cara held the sunglasses up to her face and shivered. Maybe June could read them over the phone.

"Hello?"

Suddenly all of Cara's breath was sucked away. "Hi. June?"

"Yes?"

"This is Cara Nelson."

There was a horrible pause. "Cara? This is an unlisted number. How did you get it?"

"June, I'm sorry for disturbing you at home, but I called and called at your office and always got the answering machine."

"Did Thea give you the number?"

Cara's head drummed. "Please listen. I *have* to see you again. I won't ask you about my death or anything. It's about Danny, the boy you said I'd meet. I have to know about him. It's really important."

Another pause. "Cara, you had no right to call me at home about a reading."

"But you wouldn't see me, and you wouldn't return my calls."

"That's my prerogative."

Anger washed over Cara. "No, it's not. Not when you foresaw my death and refused to talk about it. You can't just do that to someone. Everything you said has come true and now I'm in love and I'm scared and I need your help."

Nancy was whispering. "Cara, take it easy!" but

Cara was biting back tears and in no mood to listen. She heard June's breathing at the other end.

"All right," June said. "Call me at the office. Even if you get the machine, leave your name and tell me when you can see me. I'll try to fit you in."

"Thank you!" Cara said. "I really, really appreciate it."

She switched off the phone and set it down. Slipping the sunglasses back into her purse, she looked at Nancy. "Okay. Now we're getting somewhere."

"You're amazing, Cara."

She was wired now, and sleep was out of the question. Then she saw that Nancy's head was down. "You're not doing well, are you?"

Nancy shook her head. "I'll be okay."

She gently raised Nancy up and pushed back her hair. "Lie down, kid. You're not Supergirl."

"No, you are." Nancy managed a smile.

Cara eased Nancy back onto the bed, helping her lift her cast. Nancy bit her lip hard and gasped. Cara rubbed Nancy's leg above the cast. "It'll get better."

"Four more weeks."

"Listen, let me run. You need some sleep."

Looking up at her, Nancy said, "Don't you have to call your mom?"

"No. She called here and said I should come home. She must have some disaster on her hands. Probably the heater blew again."

Nancy gripped Cara's hand. "Thanks."

"Don't thank me. I got you into this mess."

"You did *not*. Stop saying that."

"Okay, okay, I'll stop saying it." She slipped her purse over her shoulder. "See you tomorrow."

"Right. You have the first draft of Graham's paper?"

"Not totally. Maybe I'll do that tonight."

Nancy folded her hands over her stomach. "You're going to flunk out and not graduate. Hey, throw me the remote, okay?"

Cara tossed the remote to Nancy, who clicked on the TV. As Nancy channel surfed, Cara waved and left. On her way out the door, she called, " 'Night, Mrs. C!"

"Good night, Cara," Mrs. Chu called back. "Be careful. Don't walk in the middle of the road!"

"Okay." With a smile, Cara let herself out.

The night air closed over her. The wind was changing; she could feel a bite of coldness coming through the soft warmth. Cara gripped her purse strap and hurried down Nancy's driveway into the street. Her back tingled as she walked.

Headlights stabbed the road. Cara turned, paralyzed, but the car rocketed past her. She stood shivering for a long time, working to breathe normally. Maybe this wasn't such a good idea.

Walking more quickly, Cara tried to block out her anxiety. Soon it would be her sweet sixteen party, and this nightmare would be over. She ached for Danny. Maybe she wouldn't call June. Maybe she'd just trust this guy who loved her.

She stopped, terrified. It was a sound, a rustling sound. Glancing around, she saw only dark lawns and lighted windows. Clouds covered the moon.

A dog, probably. She blew out a hard breath and walked very fast. Just around the corner was her block, and her house.

More rustling. Putting her head down Cara focused on the asphalt beneath her, on the dry wind, on the humid night air.

They were human footsteps! She stopped again, not knowing where to run. Someone was following her. He could be anywhere, behind any house. Cara turned toward Nancy's house. Too far away now. She had to round the corner.

Maybe that's what he had in mind. Maybe his pals were waiting there. Or *her* pals. Maybe Dyann wanted to make sure Cara was off the newspaper.

With a shake of her head, she forced herself to move. She held her breath as she turned the corner and looked down the long, hilly street. Branches overhung the road, making scary shadows. Headlights slithered over a hill and Cara backstepped into the trees. With hammering heart, she thought that this was just like the first time.

The car rattled toward her, and she shut her eyes as it passed. *Whoa, I've got it bad,* she realized. She saw that she was standing on a vacant parcel of land, thick with trees and growth.

Cara wished a house were here. She stood very still, straining to hear. No rustling. Only fifty yards and she'd be home, and next time she would *make* her mom get her.

She brushed some flying bugs from her face, then stepped toward the road. For a second she thought she must be standing in quicksand because her legs wouldn't move. Then she was jerked backward and the trees closed around her.

A scream bubbled up in her throat but something

powerful clamped down over her mouth. She was pulled back against a tree trunk and pinned there.

Fear gagged her. She heard her breath, like a hurricane wind. Silently she whimpered, *Help me, please somebody . . .*

She smelled the damp mold of the woods. Desperately, she tried to move her lips, but her face was being crushed by a hand. Why couldn't she see a face?

The moon slipped out from behind clouds then, and she saw an outline of a figure, but the head was misshapen and without features. He had a black stocking tied over his head. Cara wriggled against his grip, which was like iron.

He said, "What do you want to see last?" His voice sounded like gravel.

Her eyes flickered to his hand. He held up a hunting knife, turning it so it caught the light from the moon. How was he holding her if he had a knife in one hand?

There was someone else, someone behind her. Without thought, she thrashed against the imprisoning hands, knowing she had to escape because she couldn't die.

Coldness rippled through her arm. She screamed without sound, tearing her throat. Her shoulder throbbed. He thrust the knife in front of her face, and its tip was black with blood.

"Last look?" he said.

He'd cut her arm. There was no pain, though. She saw the moon, suddenly brilliant between branches. Coldness penetrated her body, like paralyzing venom.

He raised the knife. Cara felt herself blacking out.

Then there was another figure, arms outstretched. Cara heard a woman pleading, but no words, just a gurgling sound as if she were underwater.

It seemed to Cara that the two figures were in a movie, whispering in urgent tones. The man with the knife said something about not being ready to go all the way. Then he turned to Cara. "Soon," he said or something that sounded like it.

Now they were gone. She could see the road, past the trees. Had he killed her? If she were dead, she'd have to tell Mom.

The thought of Mom and Dad at her funeral made her cry. And Nancy, on her crutches, looking down into the grave. Cara stared up at all of them, thinking, *I'm really sorry, I screwed up*. The first shower of dirt spattered down on her and, feeling deeply sad, she thought, *Goodbye*.

CHAPTER

15

Detective Greene was a big, rumpled man in a brown suit. His thinning ochre hair needed combing. *Another redhead in my life,* Cara thought. Except this one was about as old as her dad and was asking her questions about who had stabbed her in the woods.

"You didn't see any facial features?" he asked.

She shook her head.

"Were they wearing masks?"

"I don't know. The guy was. A stocking, I think. His head was all distorted. The girl—I couldn't tell."

"You said the male was about six feet tall, the girl about five-six?"

"I guess. I really couldn't see too well."

Detective Greene scratched something out on his notepad. The coffeemaker gurgled on the counter, a sound Cara usually heard when her mom's friends came over. That was back in normal times. Now the sound mocked her. *Danny,* she thought, but Danny hadn't called.

"Okay, Cara. You've said you don't suspect any of the kids you know."

"Right."

"Are you sure?"

"Yeah, I'm sure."

Cara shuddered and clasped her hands together on the table. She imagined cops knocking on Nancy's door. *They probably suspect Mark because he just broke up with me!*

The phone rang, jarring her. She heard her mom pick it up in the bedroom. The phone hadn't *stopped* ringing since the attack. Relatives, friends, *Newsday,* Channel 12, the police, everyone. Dad had been an attack dog, protecting his little girl.

She raised her left arm to push back her hair, and nearly fainted as pain roared up her shoulder. "You okay?" Detective Greene asked.

She nodded. Carefully, she rested her wrist on the table again. Twenty-three stitches, Mom told her. "We made sure a plastic surgeon was there, so it won't be a bad scar." Too late. This scar would be there forever.

Mom came in and forced a smile. "Ready for some coffee, Detective?"

Detective Greene said, "Sure."

Scrutinizing Cara, Mom said, "Are you in pain?"

"Sort of."

"How come your arm isn't in the sling?"

"I *hate* that sling."

"I know, but if you tear the stitches, you'll just make it worse." She poured coffee into a ceramic mug and set it in front of Detective Greene. Then she pulled out a chair and sat catty-corner to Cara. "Honey, I know it's killing you, but I want it to heal."

"Me too."

"Cara, this is horrible for all of us. I know you're a loyal friend. But if you know anything, *anything,* you have to share it. You can't be loyal to someone who would do this to you."

Cara felt detached. The past couple of days had been like a weird music video, with images overlapping. She sort of remembered waking up in the hospital and she sort of remembered Mom and Dad peering down at her, and then she was home with people all over the house, and her class photo on a TV screen. Mostly she remembered how much it hurt, how she kept waking up at night with her arm on fire. They gave her painkillers which cooked her brain. Today was the first day she could function at all.

Except she *couldn't* function. She couldn't think, or plan, or make a decision. She just sat in front of the TV and watched whatever was on. Sometimes she broke into hysterical sobbing. The rest of the time she curled up inside herself, feeling nothing.

"Cara?" Mom prompted.

She shook her head. "I'm sorry I'm not helping. I don't know anyone who'd do this. I mean who'd do this to *anybody.*"

Detective Greene sipped coffee and clunked the mug down on the table. "You were attacked in the woods at the end of the block." Detective Greene squinted down at his notes. "A call came to your friend's house. Someone saying she was your mother asked you to come home."

"Right." Cara remembered her mom saying, "I never called you, never."

"So the girl who called you was probably the girl in the woods."

"I guess so."

"Which means she knew you were at Nancy's house."

"I guess so."

"Is there anyone you're not getting along with?" Detective Greene asked. "Fighting over a boyfriend? Jealousy?"

"What about that strange boy in your health class," Mom said. "Eddie something?"

"Eddie Belmonte? I don't even talk to him."

"Well, you said he was strange."

Detective Greene looked up. "I know about Eddie Belmonte. He's a character."

"Has he ever done anything like this?" Mom asked.

"I wouldn't put it past him," Detective Greene said. "He's already been booked for vandalism, burglary, malicious mischief. He's been in therapy half his life from what I know. Sick kid."

Mom looked at Cara. "You never had any contact with him?"

"No!"

"I wasn't trying to insult you."

Leaning back, Cara glanced at the spring brightness outside. "He never talks to anybody."

"Does he do *crazy* things?" Mom asked.

Laughing softly, Cara said, "All the time."

Detective Greene asked, "Does he have a girlfriend?"

"Not likely."

"Why not?" Detective Greene asked.

"Because it would be too *gross*. Who'd want to go near him?"

Detective Greene drank a huge gulp of coffee and glanced at his watch. "No problems with friends?"

"What about that girl Dyann?" Mom asked. "The one you don't get along with."

Detective Greene asked, "Dyann who?"

"Nobody."

Mom lost it. "Cara, this isn't a game. You got twenty-three stitches in your arm. Someone dragged you into the woods and cut you up. I don't understand you!"

"No, you don't," Cara said.

In the embarrassed silence, Detective Greene asked, "Want to talk about her?"

Cara sighed. "Dyann Wilson. She lives with her mom, but she wants to be in the city with her dad. That's about all I know."

"And you don't get along?"

Cara felt caged. "It's no big deal. She wrote this editorial for the school paper, about athletics getting more money than arts. The jocks got on her case and she's like super sensitive. She blamed me for not protecting her."

"You think she might want to get back at you?"

Detective Greene had big pores all over his face, especially on his nose. "I doubt it," Cara said. "She falls apart when you look at her the wrong way. Anyway, she did the whole April newspaper, so she's pretty happy."

"Anything else?" Detective Greene asked.

"No. She's not a threat."

Not a threat, just someone so important that June mixed them up. *You're so closely woven together. She is urgently joined with your destiny. I've never experienced such closeness—it's like a single heartbeat.*

And there was something else June had said. *I was reading a very negative emotion . . . an unthinking cruelty. It was coming from the driver of the car who hit your father.*

Unthinking cruelty. The kind of cruelty that would make someone run down Nancy, or put a black widow spider in Cara's book bag, or cut her with a knife. It was such a crazy thing for June to say. Some drunk hit Daddy. That's what everyone assumed.

Or some psycho who wanted to hurt Daddy and who wanted to hurt his daughter.

But that couldn't be Dyann. Dyann didn't know Cara until this year.

"Cara?" Mom's voice, concerned.

"Sorry."

Detective Greene drained the coffee mug. "I'll get going. If there's nobody you want us to talk to, we'll pursue the investigation as best we can."

"I'm sorry," Cara said. "I don't know people like this."

He stood up, looking even bigger. "We have some blood samples, and we have some fabric and hair samples we're running through the lab."

"They're probably mine," Cara said. "I was the one shoved against the tree."

"You're probably right. We'll call when we know something."

Mom implored Detective Greene, "Can't she have police protection? Someone's obviously after her."

Detective Greene snapped his notepad shut. "There's not enough to warrant a guard on her. Nobody actually tried to kill her—"

"You don't call this attempted murder?"

"He cut her arm. He didn't try to stab her in any vital area, and he didn't cut her twice."

"She could have bled to death," Mom protested.

"No severed arteries."

"And the spider? That wasn't an attempt on her life?"

As he sidled toward the door, Detective Greene said, "That was more like a prank. All the incidents could be considered pranks that went too far."

Mom stood up, disgusted. "Give me a break."

"Sorry," Detective Greene said. "I know it sounds lousy, but unless there's a note, a phone threat, some clear intention to kill her, we can't give her protection. Just be careful for a while. Make sure she gets driven everywhere. Keep her home at night."

"Thanks a lot," Cara said.

Detective Greene shrugged. "We'll do our best to find this guy. Call me if you think of anything that will help."

He twisted the doorknob and went out, letting in a stream of cool air. Cara listened to his car door open and close, and the sound of his engine roaring. Mom rinsed the mug. "Why don't you go lie down for a while?"

"I've been lying down."

"Well, I think you're still pretty weary. Come on. I'll bring in a pizza later."

"You've been bringing in pizza for days."

Laughing, Mom dried her hands. "Brian and Andrea wanted to come back but we told them not to."

"Well, they'll be here for the party. It's less than a week away."

Mom put down the dish towel. "Cara, you're not serious."

Her heart beating fast, Cara stood up. "Of course I'm serious. We're not going to cancel that party."

"May I remind you that two people dragged you into the woods and assaulted you with a knife! Things aren't exactly normal."

"I know that," Cara said. "But I still want the party."

Mom put her hands on Cara's elbows. "I know you want it. But things have changed. You're in deadly danger. The most important thing in the world now is to protect you until we find out who's doing this."

"He won't crash my party, Mom!"

"Cara, I'm not worrying about a party now. Come to your senses."

"I *am* at my senses," Cara cried. She writhed out of her mother's grip and hugged herself. "I'm not becoming a prisoner in my house because some jerk is out there plotting his next move. Let him come to the party. He can get arrested there."

Shaking, she realized she could pass out. She *had* to speak to June, she had to know.

"Cara, you're talking nonsense."

So talk sense. Tell her!

About what? About the prediction? She hadn't even told her mom about breaking up with Mark.

Would Mark drag her into the woods and cut her?

Not Mark. Someone with unthinking cruelty. Did Dyann have unthinking cruelty? Who would help her do stuff like this anyway? Eddie Belmonte? Did Dyann know Eddie? Someone said he kept looking at her in English class. So what? Dyann was attractive in a bizarre way.

Eddie never talked to Cara. He never went near her, except that time in Mr. Harris's class when he charged up the aisle and brushed past her.

Past her book bag.

Yeah, right. Eddie dropped a spider into her book bag because he hated her with unthinking cruelty. This was getting nowhere. She had to see June.

Mom gently touched Cara's back. "Come on, honey. Get some rest."

The pain spiraled into her throat. Huddling, she begged. "I want my party. Please, Mom. Please."

Cara's cheek rested against the soft fabric of Mom's T-shirt, and she smelled Mom's damp skin as she cried. "We'll talk later," Mom said soothingly.

Cara let Mom walk her to her room. She dropped onto her bed and stared mindlessly at her stuffed animals, while Mom shut the blinds. The room fell into amber shadow and Cara truly felt imprisoned, shut away from sunlight, from friends, from everything she'd ever known.

In her black bedroom, Dyann listened to electronic music and waited for Eddie to pick her up. Mother would be home in a couple of hours and she had to get drunk, puke, and recover by then.

Closing her eyes, she imagined the knife stabbing deep into Cara until she bled her life out. And then Mark Lanier and Joey Bianco and Carl Ward. And Mother.

Then she'd go home and find her friends. They'd dance, ten thousand of them under the Fifty-ninth Street Bridge, and she'd celebrate her life again.

Dyann lay back down. Next time she wouldn't stop him. Next time she'd be ready to do it all.

CHAPTER

16

In the bookroom, Cara studied her math while Mrs. Harris typed at the computer. It felt good to be there again.

"Cara," Mrs. Harris said suddenly. "How do I make a paragraph back up?"

"Back up?"

"Yes. So it's part of the paragraph before it."

"Oh. You just keep pressing Delete."

"Oh. Really?" Mrs. Harris tapped the key. "Thank you."

"No prob." Cara folded her arms across the bottom half of the book and tried again to understand the formulas. Never in her life had she missed this much school. She kept thinking how she hadn't called June yet. Cara Nelson Avoids Challenge. Hold the front page.

Whoops. She didn't want to think about the *Tempest* meeting today.

The clunky old printer started rattling. Mrs. Harris watched the screen for a moment, then stood. "Are you going to be all right here?"

"I've got a pass to leave class five minutes early." She fished in her purse and held it up. "See?"

Mrs. Harris smiled. "Aren't you supposed to be wearing an arm sling?"

"You're just like my mom!" She dug in her book bag and pulled out the blue sling. "There."

"Wouldn't it do more good on your arm?"

"Yes." She dropped it on the table. "I just hate wearing it."

The printer stopped rattling and Mrs. Harris meticulously peeled off the pinfeed holes. "I have to get my lunch." She slung her pocketbook over a plump shoulder. "I think it's terrible what happened to you."

"So do I."

Mrs. Harris looked at Cara with great tenderness, then went out. Cara stood up, folding over a corner of the math book page. *Don't think about it.* When she was scared, that's how she did the impossible.

She went to the phone and punched in June's office number. After the recorded message, she spoke. "Hi, June, it's Cara Nelson. I'm calling like you said, for an appointment. Call me back at *this* number, *not* at my home number." Cara read the school number from the phone.

A shadow passed across the door glass. Cara glimpsed raincoat and sunglasses.

Shaking, she hung up. That *couldn't* have been Eddie. He had no reason to watch her. Shivering, she fumbled for the sling and put it on.

* * *

Cara hung out after the buses left. She liked the school after hours. Cheerleaders hurried to buy a bagel before practice. Student government kids decorated a showcase. Until now, Cara had owned this after-school world.

Hoisting her book bag, she made a right turn at the main staircase. And saw Danny.

For a second, she thought she was mistaking someone else for him. Then he hurried toward her, lanky and smiling in a black shirt and light jeans.

She half said his name and then he whipped an arm around the back of her neck. She let her book bag slide from her shoulder and thud to the floor as she kissed him. She didn't care that they'd be seen. She didn't want to be away from him again, ever.

His eyes swept her face and her bad arm. "Baby, I'm so sorry," he said.

"Where were you?" she demanded.

"Nowhere. I heard about it, but I couldn't get near you. Too many people around."

"Nobody's more important than you, Danny. I couldn't care less about anyone else."

Smiling, he tousled her hair. "I didn't want your parents asking you questions, or people looking at me when I came over. I figured I'd try here, but when the buses were gone, I thought I'd missed you."

"No, you didn't miss me." She rested her cheek against his shirt. "Oh, man, it's good to see you."

"Good to see you too."

He walked her back to the stairway and sat on a stair as she leaned against the wall. She couldn't stop looking at him. He asked her about the attack and she told him the whole story, all of it, while his eyes narrowed and his breathing got faster. She was crying when she finished.

"I don't know what to say," he told her. "I'm blown away."

"Yeah, that's kind of how I feel."

He ran the back of his hand down her cheek and over her lips. She tenderly kissed his fingers.

"Any idea who this clown is?"

She shook her head. "No."

"The girl?"

"My mom thinks it's Dyann Wilson."

"Who's she?"

"A very weird person, not the killer type." Something popped into her head. "I just realized something! The way she spells her name, it's a mixed up version of *your* name. D-y-a-n-n, and D-a-n-n-y. That's cool."

"I guess so."

Cara gripped his hand. "You're not her long lost brother, are you? Or long lost *lover?*"

"Don't think so."

"Come upstairs with me, Danny."

"What's upstairs?"

"My friends."

His eyebrows went up. "You want me to meet them?"

"Yeah. And I want to do something else. Please? I have to do this right now."

He searched her eyes. "Wherever you lead, I'll follow."

"I love you."

"I love you too."

She swallowed hard and said, "Come on."

He carried her book bag and she nearly dragged him through the corridor to the *Tempest* office. She heard their voices. Turning to Danny, she said, "Stay with me."

"They're not armed and dangerous, are they?"

Laughing, she said, "No!"

She led him into the room and thought her heart would come flying through her chest. Nick saw her first and waved. "Cara!"

She stood in the doorway of the office, and felt a gentle ache, as for a friend long dead. Thea was at one of the MACs, working on a layout.

"Hi, Cara," she said. "How are you?"

"Hurting," Cara said. "How's it going?"

"Pretty well."

"Dyann's outrageous," Nick said, with his usual tact. "She's teaching us how to do layout and she's going to get color for the next issue!"

Cara felt her heart clutch. "How are you managing that on our budget?"

"We're getting in some ads that will pay for it— thanks to Thea."

"Way to go, Thea."

"It's an ad for a tanning salon," Nick said. "Just in time for the prom."

"Great," Cara said. "Look good and get cancer all for one low price."

"It's money in the bank, right?"

Cara wasn't prepared for Dyann to be so in control. Nick's mention of the prom resonated in her blood. She thought of getting out of a white limo, on Danny's arm. Which made her realize that Danny was hiding just out of sight. What was he afraid of?

"Who's with you, Cara? I hear breathing," Nick said.

"Danny, you can show yourself."

Danny stepped into the doorway, sliding an arm around Cara's waist. The room quieted. "Hi," Danny said.

"Guys, this is Danny Schonberg. Danny, this is Nick and Thea."

"Nice meeting you," Nick muttered. Thea reddened.

"Do you go to this school?" Nick asked.

Danny said, "Only when I have someone important to see."

"We have to run," Cara said. "I'll catch you guys later."

Nick asked, "Are you ever coming back to the paper, Cara?"

"I don't think so. Not this year, anyway. I'm like really backed up with work, and I'm still a mess. You can do it, Nick."

"Well, Dyann's really got it working."

"Where is she?" Cara asked.

"Conferring with Mr. Brill," Nick answered.

Another blow to her ego. "Have fun," Cara said. "You too."

Danny said, "Nice meeting you." Then he said, "Anybody need a lift home?"

Cara stared at him. Nick said, "No, I have my car. Thea, you want to go with them?"

Thea shook her head rapidly. "I'm getting picked up at three-thirty."

"Okay," Danny said. "Take care." He guided

Cara from the room with subtle pressure at the small of her back.

As they walked down the corridor, Cara asked, "Why did you offer rides?"

He shrugged. "Seemed like a nice thing to do."

"Thanks. I would have *loved* having Thea in the car."

"She seems pretty quiet."

"Spooky is the word." Sunlight pressed against the windows. She felt a headache coming on. "Don't do that again, okay?"

"Getting possessive?"

"Come on, Danny, I don't want to fight. I'm so happy you're here."

He grabbed her around the neck again. "No fights."

She wriggled out of his unpleasant grip, wondering why he was suddenly hurting her. Maybe she was just depressed about quitting the *Tempest*. Maybe Danny couldn't do *anything* to make her feel better.

"Where do you want to go?" she asked.

'Well—" He glanced at his watch. "How about I buy you an ice-cream cone at Friendly's and then take you home?"

"That's *it?*"

"I know. Short date. But I have to get somewhere by four. Like I said, I just stopped by. I'll call you later."

"I've heard that before," she said as they clattered down the stairs.

That night Nancy came over, and for a couple of hours it was heaven. They played Scrabble and listened to tapes and Nancy leaned on one crutch and helped Cara clean out her bureau drawers. Except for the stiff ache in Cara's arm, it was almost like it used to be.

"So you're really serious about Danny?" Nancy asked as she held up a sweatshirt.

"I don't know," Cara said. "He was different today. Don't ask me how, he just was."

"How was he different?" Nancy asked.

Cara said, "I told you not to ask me how—" Then she got it, and slapped Nancy with a halter top.

"You think he's cheating on you?"

"How could he be cheating on me?" Cara said. "We're not even going out yet. We just ride around." She stuffed a tank top back into a drawer. "Did you know his name is a mixed up version of Dyann's name?"

"Huh?"

"Yeah. D-a-n-n-y and D-y-a-n-n. Cool, huh?"

"Strange, but true." Nancy made weird noises.

"Stop! What do you call that, anyway?"

"Underwear," Nancy said, peering into the drawer.

"No, fudgebrain. When you mix up the letters of a word and get another word?"

Nancy dropped the top she was holding and sat down on Cara's bed. "I know what you mean. I learned this in English once."

Cara felt dizzy from effort as she leaned against the dresser. "We're a great pair. The walking wounded."

"Tell me about it."

"Okay. It all started when this guy ran us down in his car—"

"All right, all right!" Nancy brandished her crutch.

They laughed. Not that it helped much. The depression was always there, like a tumor in her heart.

"Anagram!" Nancy shouted.

"Huh?"

Cara's phone rang. Nancy said, "Anagram. That's what that thingie is called."

"What thingie?"

"When you mix up letters and get another word. Are you going to answer the stupid phone?"

"Oh, right! Anagram!" Cara picked up her phone. "Yeah?"

"Cara? This is Nick."

"Nick?" Something was wrong, because Nick never called her. "What's up?"

"Have you heard from Thea?"

"No. Why would I hear from her?"

"I don't know, but we're calling everyone."

A cold dread sucked out Cara's breath. "Nick, what's wrong?"

"Well, Thea's mom came but Thea wasn't waiting for her. Nobody knows where she is."

Nancy asked what was wrong and Cara shushed her. "What do you mean nobody knows where she is?"

"She's missing. I just wondered if you'd heard anything."

Cara said, "No. I didn't hear anything. She probably went home with a friend."

"*Thea?*"

"Okay, I know. I hope she turns up."

"Me too."

Cara hung up. Nancy said, "What's happening, Cara?"

"Thea's missing. She wasn't waiting for her mom."

The room almost rang with tension. Cara went to her window and stared into the night. Why Thea? Because Thea was June's niece, and the psycho didn't want Cara to see June again.

Get real. Thea was just lost.

Or raped. Or killed.

The night seemed to press in, like a smothering shroud. Cara turned and stared at Nancy, who stared at her. "I'm scared," Cara said.

"I'm sleeping here tonight," Nancy whispered.

"I'm never sleeping again." Cara looked bleakly at the telephone and thought *I'm going to die*.

CHAPTER

17

June realized her hand was trembling as she poured hot water into her teacup. She clutched the handle of the pot more tightly and pulled in a long breath. *Today is her party.*

Sipping from the cup, June walked to the front door and looked out at the courtyard between apartment buildings. On days like this she missed Hal. He loved spring days.

Impulsively, June walked back to her desk and lifted the photo of Thea. The girl looked darkly pretty in it, against the out-of-focus tree branches.

June set down the photo and bit her lip. Dyann Wilson had begged Thea to go with her for newspaper supplies, just before three-thirty. Dyann said she needed Thea to ride along because she had just gotten her license and needed moral support. Two or three wrong turns and they were "lost," on a winding road on the North Shore. Dyann stopped at a grocery store and came out with directions and the assurance that she'd called Thea's mother. Then back on the road, farther and farther they went, out to the East End.

June sat at her desk, sifting the story. Out in Orient Point, Dyann stopped again, presumably made another call, got directions back. By the time she brought Thea home, the police were out looking for her.

Thea's mother had called, frantic about her daughter. "Please find her." June had sensed Thea far out on the Island, and a girl with her. Soon, she understood everything.

Now June saw the party, and Cara, petite and lovely in her dress. Her poor arm was still bandaged, but she was dancing gamely with her friend Nancy, as everyone applauded the two wounded girls. June could smell the food, could see the lights spinning.

She could see *him*, too, more and more clearly. She knew he could kill. She'd known it from the first time she sensed him as the one who'd injured Cara's father.

"You have no place in other people's heads," her husband, Hal, had told her before he died.

"I *do*," she'd answered. "Readings can help people. I don't tell them they're going to die." She'd smiled and kissed his chin. "They know that, anyway."

No, not always. June had turned away from Cara. Too old to take risks, too selfish to disrupt her life.

She'd never see Hal again, but she could help someone who needed her now. As a child shrieked outside in play, June went into her bedroom to get dressed.

* * *

Dyann viciously zapped the TV in her room and it blinked off. Gripping the controller in one hand, she flopped back on her bed and thought about Cara's party.

Happy birthday to me, she recited. When was her birthday, a little over two weeks ago? Grandma had sent a card. Daddy probably had, too, but Mother would tear it up.

Eddie had given her a single rose.

She got up, too hyper to rest. She wanted to crash the party and annoy Cara. He'd said no. She looked at the rose, in a slim vase on her dresser. But *in* the dresser— With a warm bubbling in her throat, she opened her underwear drawer, slipped her hands beneath the silk and cotton, and drew out the knife.

She flipped the stereo on; a tape was already loaded and slammed her with its driving beat. She moved sensuously, turning the knife around and around. Its tip gleamed, cleaned of blood. She'd begged him to let her have it for a while.

In a sudden passion she thrust the knife blade upward, imagining Cara to be there. A little embarrassed, she hid the knife again, and moved restlessly around her room.

Her phone jingled. She turned off the stereo and pounced. "Hello?"

"Where are you?"

"Here. In my room. Where are *you?*"

"Never mind. Did you get rid of the knife?"

She hesitated, glancing at the drawer. "Not yet."

He sighed. "Pretty stupid, right?"

"Okay. I'll do it."

"I'm going over there now."

The pressure on her chest tightened. She curled up on her bed, twining the phone wire around her wrist. "Okay."

"Feeling good?"

"Yes." She was trembling. "Eddie, she's going to die?"

"How far can you go?"

The words came hard. "All the way."

"You'll like how it feels. It's a rush. Ultimate control."

"Where are you taking her?"

"Can't say. Just wait for me."

The doorbell rang. Dyann nearly exploded with tension. "Someone's at the door, Eddie."

"Wait for me."

She hung up and stood with clenched fists as the doorbell rang again. She needed to be drunk, really drunk.

A third ring. Dyann rattled open her bureau drawer, took out the knife, and sheathed it in the waistband of her shorts. The metal blade chilled her stomach.

Downstairs, the house floated with dust motes and sunbeams. She opened the door and a woman stood there. "Yeah?"

"Dyann?"

"Who are you?"

"June Brady."

Thea's aunt. Dyann tried to think. She'd prepped herself for almost anybody, but not her. "What do you want?"

"Just to talk for a while."

"About what?"

175

June stared hard at her, and Dyann cast her eyes down. "You know about what, Dyann."

Dyann skulked inside the doorway. "My mother is coming back from shopping soon and she's going to be pissed if I let someone in."

June smiled as she stepped inside. "Your mother is at a friend's house, having coffee. A gray house with green shutters. In South Beach, about a half hour away."

"You're crazy." Dyann backed up and knelt on the couch, her hair falling in front of her eye.

June sat opposite her, in a wing chair. "Let's talk about Thea and a long car ride."

"Why?"

"Why not?" June leaned slightly forward and Dyann's breathing thickened. "Let's talk about Eddie too. Okay?"

"I don't know what you mean," Dyann said, as her hand slipped to her side, and rubbed against the knife.

The thing that got to Cara most was how *hot* it was in here. She wriggled between bodies as she headed for Mom and Dad's table. Along the way she traded high-fives with friends and off-center kisses with relatives.

Mom and Dad both sat at the table. Afternoon light glowed through the leaded window behind them. Mom eyed Cara with concern. "How are you doing?"

Cara perched at the edge of a chair. The deejay played a soft, slow song since everyone was eating. "Great."

"Are you sure?"

"Yeah, really."

"You look wiped out."

"Hardly." Cara's body was being held together by rubber bands. Her legs wobbled when she walked. Didn't matter. The party was here, her friends were here, the deejay was here. Every time the fear came up, she pushed it back down.

It was sort of working, but he'd killed a lot of it for her, and she wished him dead for that.

Dad eyed her, trying to swallow ziti so he could talk. "Watch your arm."

"I'm watching it," She'd festooned an Ace bandage with gold tinsel. The pain hammered up into her shoulder and across the back of her neck, but she was living with it.

"Is the food to your liking?" Mom asked.

Cara laughed. "Yeah. He gave us everything."

Cara felt someone behind her and turned to see her sister, Andrea. "Hi, peanut," Andrea said.

"Hi, scummo." Andrea was Dad's child, tall and big-boned. With her blond hair swept up, she looked pretty cool.

"Neat party," Andrea said.

"Listen, when do you have to go back?"

"Wednesday."

"I want to go clubbing with you."

"I beg your pardon?" Mom said.

"Eighteen and under," Cara said.

Andrea smirked. "Let's do it. I miss you."

Cara basked in the warmth of the moment. Having Andrea here, and Brian, and partying today made everything else like a bad dream. Maybe he'd stop coming after her. Maybe he'd had enough.

The music changed suddenly, to the opening strains of "That's What Friends Are For." A screech of excitement swept around the room as her friends rushed to the tiny dance floor to link arms and sway. Nancy materialized at the table, along with Patty and Joanne.

"Come on!" Nancy shouted over the music.

Cara mouthed to Mom and Dad, "I love you guys." She got up, Andrea gently placing a hand at her elbow. She looked into Andrea's worried eyes. "Thanks, scummo."

"No prob, peanut."

With a rush of emotion, Cara hugged Andrea, who grabbed her close and held on. Then Cara broke loose, feeling wetness on her face. She threw a smile at Andrea as the girls dragged her to the dance floor.

Swept up by the others, she moved back and forth in her stockinged feet, one arm around Patty's waist, one arm around Nancy's. Nancy leaned on one crutch while Joanne hung on to her. They faced another row of friends, and behind them, the adults. Cara sang as loudly as she could, and they all laughed and swayed harder.

Cara stole a look at Nancy, who grinned back and lifted her crutch victoriously. Everyone whooped and Cara pumped her fist in the air. Nancy yelled, "Mighty Mite rules!"

Cara laughed. For a second she remembered that Mark wasn't there. There wouldn't be any slow dance while the lights spun.

Not with Danny, either.

No bad thoughts! Defiantly she screamed out the words to the song.

The deejay pumped up the volume, and the loving chain of friends broke into wild gyrations. Cara saw her father cross the room and a question raced through her mind.

"Daddy!" She slipped out of the dancing crowd and caught him by the arm. He looked handsome in his gray suit, except his tie was tied too tight.

"Hi, baby."

"Don't get lost in the john! I'm cutting the cake soon."

"Don't worry."

She didn't know why but all at once she asked, "Daddy do you know Eddie Belmonte?"

He gave her an odd look. "He's some weird kid from your school?"

"Yeah. Do you know him?"

With a shake of his head, Dad said, "Never heard of him."

"You never hired him to help you tile floors or anything?"

It was hard to hear over the music. "Nope. His name doesn't sound familiar."

"Did you ever fire any kid you worked with?"

"Why are you asking this stuff?"

"No reason."

Suddenly she felt nervous. Daddy said, "You think this kid is the one who's been after you?"

"No," Cara said. "I don't really know him either."

"So why do you think I know him?"

She shrugged. "I was just asking. Be back here for the big dance!"

He smiled but looked troubled. Cara stood watching the dancing. It would have fit. If Eddie was out for revenge, she believed he'd run down the man who fired him.

Eddie Belmonte. She half hummed the name as the music pounded. What was it about his name?

"Cara."

With a gasp, she spun and whipped her shoulder around too fast. Joanne stared at her, horrified. "Oh God, are you okay? I didn't mean to scare you."

"It's okay. What's up?"

"There's a *guy* out in the parking lot who wants to see you?"

"Huh?"

"Yeah. Some kid came to the door and I happened to be out in that little lobby thingie—"

"The vestibule."

"Yeah. Anyway, he said to tell you to come out."

Her stomach clutched. "Did he give his name? What did he look like?"

"This wasn't the guy, just some kid. He said you'd know who it was."

Her throat pulsed so hard she thought she'd hurl. She knew it was Danny. "Okay," Cara said. "Listen, if anyone wants me, tell them I'll be right back."

Joanne's eyes narrowed. "You'd better. I heard the deejay say they were bringing out the cake in two minutes."

"That's what I'll be. Two minutes."

She patted Joanne's arm and hurried toward the entrance. How selfish to dump her friends and family just to see Danny. But Danny was going to save her today.

CHAPTER
18

Golden light flooded the parking lot. For a moment Cara stopped and drank it in. Then she remembered why she was out here. Shivering, she scanned the cars crowding the lot, but didn't see Danny's Toyota.

With a glance back at the catering hall, Cara wove a path among the cars, moving toward the rear of the lot. Finally she reached a stockade fence overhung with trees. She hurried along the fence, finding herself on the sidewalk.

"Danny?" she called. Feeling silly, she looked right and left. The kid must have been pranking.

Cara felt disappointed. As she started back, an engine roared. Cara turned and saw the headlights of a black panel truck. The truck was dented, with rust along its rocker panels. Breathing away her fright, Cara turned back.

The truck honked. She looked again, this time at the windshield. Danny was in the driver's seat.

She made a puzzled face. Danny opened the cab door and dropped to the ground. "Like it?" he asked.

"What is it?"

"A truck."

Smiling, she walked toward him. "I can see that. What happened to the Toyota?"

"Mom needed it. Her car got stolen in the Roosevelt Field parking lot."

"So you have a mother, eh?"

She reached him and he pulled her close to kiss her. "Yes, I do."

"And maybe an address and a phone number?"

"Maybe." His eyes were moving around, searching for someone. "How's the party?"

"It's fantastic. Why don't you come in?"

He shook his head. "Can't. I have to show you something."

She felt a little shiver of worry in her stomach. "What's wrong?"

"Nothing too bad. Come on."

She followed him around the side of the truck, which shook as it idled. "Where did you get this thing?"

"Friend of mine. Gorgeous, huh?"

"Yeah. Beautiful."

He twisted the handle and wrenched the back door open. "Look in there."

Cara felt silly out here in her party dress. "At what?"

"Just look."

Curious, Cara peered into the back of the truck. She saw quilted padding lining the sides, and a grate in the wall that separated the cargo area from the cab. "I just see truck."

Danny tousled her hair. "You have to get in."

"What?"

"In the truck. To see."

Something cold flickered in her head. It wasn't a thought, really, more like a *concept*. "To see *what*? Danny, this is crazy. I've got to go back and cut my cake. Everyone's going to wonder where I am."

He nodded. "Yeah. I know."

She felt herself being lifted with a sudden violent motion. Then she pitched forward. Instinctively, she spread out her hands and shut her eyes. She skidded on the floor of the truck and heard a metallic slam. Darkness engulfed her. The stink of gasoline rushed into her nose.

She heard another slam and the clash of gears. The truck jerked forward and then accelerated, rocking from side to side. Cara realized the coldness in her brain was June trying to warn her.

She tried to pull herself to a sitting position. Beneath the engine noise, she heard the harsh thump of tires on road. "Danny!" she screamed. "Danny, what the hell are you doing?"

"Hang on," he said from the driver's seat.

Cara sat crumpled in a corner of the truck, prevented from movement by the speed and sway of the vehicle. "Danny, I have to get back to my party. This is crazy."

"Forget the party," he said.

She felt panic gripping her neck. "Danny, come on! Stop it."

"Sorry."

"Danny!" She heard herself scream and smash her

fists against the wall. She didn't know how long she freaked out; it just went on and on.

The truck was going very fast. She thought of Mom and Dad, of Andrea and Nancy. Waiting for her.

Help them, June!

She forced her breathing to slow. He had to stop somewhere. He had to run out of gas. Then she'd pound and pound.

On the padding.

Bleakly, she stared at the quilting. He'd put it there. He'd brought the truck to shove her in. Why?

"Danny," she called. Her voice was a rasp.

"Yeah?"

She began to cry. "What's going on? Please?"

"Taking you somewhere."

"Where?"

"You'll see."

"Danny, what is this?"

"Stay loose, Babe. Long ride."

"No." She freaked again, but she had no strength for it. Soon she curled up on the truck floor, whimpering.

How could she have fallen for him? How could she not *question* why he came out of nowhere, never let her see where he lived? Twenty years old, in love with a fifteen-year-old runt. Sure, it made tons of sense.

But it was predicted, and Cara had wanted to believe it. Now it had all come true. Danny had come to her party and taken her away. Except he was the one who would kill her. Desperately alone, Cara cried in the darkness of the truck.

* * *

June wondered if Cara had felt her warning. There was no way to know. But this little snip sitting opposite her was really impatient, and waiting for someone—not her mother. That meant what June had originally seen was accurate. This boy was going after Cara.

"Who are you waiting for?" June asked.

Dyann fidgeted on the couch. "Nobody."

"This is silly, Dyann. I know you're involved. I know you drove Thea around for hours to scare me. You're in a lot of trouble right now."

"I got lost," she said.

"Hardly." June felt a disturbing uneasiness throughout her body. Had something happened already? "You know who did all these things to Cara, don't you?"

"Drop dead."

"Nice mouth. Maybe I should slap it."

Dyann glared at her. "Go ahead. I'll kick your ass."

June curled her fingers around the arms of the chair. "You won't get my goat, Dyann. I've already called the police, so you're not going anywhere today."

Dyann shot to her feet. "Where are they?"

"The police? I'm sure I don't know."

"You know everything, you hag. Where did you tell them to go?"

She'd hit paydirt, but Dyann was unstable. "Why does it matter? Unless you're expecting your boyfriend here. Are you?"

"Don't screw around with me. I'll cut out your heart."

"I think you're a troubled girl, Dyann. I don't think you're a murderer."

"I'm whatever I have to be."

"Wrong." June sat up straighter. She felt terrible, the way she felt when she was getting a flu. Something *had* happened. He'd struck, and she'd missed it. Dyann had diverted her. "He's been calling the shots all along, hasn't he? What's he promised you? Money? Eternal love?"

Dyann rushed to the front door. She banged her fists softly against it, staring wildly through the glass. Then she turned and leaned against it. "Why don't you leave?"

"I'm not going anywhere."

"You're trespassing," Dyann said. "Maybe I'll call the cops."

"Go ahead."

The girl was shivering. June sensed her alcohol dependency. He had liquor with him. That's why she was so anxious for him to arrive. This was deadly serious now. June had to know for certain if Cara was gone from the party, and she had to be certain of who to look for.

Dyann shook her hair back. "Aren't you worried about Thea now?"

"No," June said. "I know where she is."

"But you won't always know where she is. Not every hour of every day."

Smiling, June said, "Don't try to sound melodramatic. You make a poor villainess."

June focused on her. Dyann didn't know where Cara was, *or* her boyfriend. June read fear and frustration and a growing sense of betrayal. He may have double-crossed her.

But she was picking up the boy, more clearly than ever. Dyann must be wearing something of his. June could see a condo, in a sprawling development. She saw a fleshy woman, Italian, with a trace of an accent. And a man, stocky, with peppery hair and a sweet smile. He was disabled somehow.

"Where does he live?" June asked.

Dyann's eyes sparked as she turned back. "What?"

"The boy you're waiting for."

Dyann rubbed her thighs nervously. "What are you talking about?"

June was picking up so many images now. A green car. A beige Toyota wagon. Dyann in the green car but not in the wagon. "He's not just in your class at school. He's your boyfriend."

"Shut up."

"I can sense it, Dyann. It's all over you. I see his house, his parents. He's bringing you liquor, isn't he?"

Dyann paced the room. "Get the hell out of my head."

"No, I don't think so. He was the one who hit Nancy, wasn't he? And put the spider in Cara's book bag, and slashed her in the woods?"

"Ask him."

"You were in the woods with him too, weren't you?" June had just realized it. She could almost smell the damp loam and see the moonlight. She was also going too far without a cop or an attorney.

Dyann rubbed her left thigh almost obsessively now. Her eyes darted around the room, as if searching for something. "I don't have to talk to you. I don't have to say anything to you."

No, she didn't. Right then June had to leave and contact the police. She had to warn Cara and have Dyann properly arrested. The girl would run but she had no car and the boy was nowhere close.

June stood. "You don't have many choices, sweetheart. You ought to think about the best deal you can cut for yourself, and about how to stop Eddie from doing anything really dumb."

"Where are you going?" Dyann asked.

"To see Cara. I'd suggest you don't run anywhere."

Dyann's chest heaved beneath her black top. "You're not going."

Only slightly worried, June said, "I don't think you're big enough to stop me, Dyann. Anyway, you just told me to leave."

June quickened her pace toward the door. Dyann cut her off. "Don't."

"Dyann, move away from the door."

"No."

With a grunt, June dug her fingers into Dyann's thin arm and tried to push her aside. She half saw Dyann's hand go to her thigh again. She glimpsed a flash of midriff and then something in Dyann's hand.

"You're crazy!" she began to cry and then a cold fire blazed in her stomach.

Nancy hobbled a few more steps across the parking lot to scan the rows of cars. "This is so weird," Nancy said. "Where did she go?"

"I told you," Joanne said. "This kid said some guy wanted to talk to her."

"And she went?"

"Yeah. She acted like she was expecting him."

"Danny."

"Who?"

Nancy leaned on her crutch, ignoring the ache in her leg. "This guy she's been seeing."

"You mean she got another guy already?"

"Uh-huh. I never met him, but Thea saw him in school."

"So where is he?"

"That's what I'd like to know." Nancy shuddered with guilt for not staying with Cara. "She wouldn't just go off with him."

"Well, you never know," Joanne said. "You do weird things when you're in love."

"Not this weird." Nancy shook her head. The sky had reddened, with black clouds at the horizon. Streetlights glowed against the sunset. "I don't know what to tell her mom and dad."

Joanne added, "The cake is sitting there and everyone's waiting."

Nancy sighed. "Well, she's not out here. We'd better go in and say something."

Dyann sat on the stairs and looked at the bottle in her hand. The vodka was in her brain now, numbing it. No more feeling in her hands. No more feeling anywhere.

She kept retching, but nothing else came up. Helplessly, she stared at the form sprawled near the front door. Dyann couldn't see the blood from here. She only remembered it. And the *feeling* of the knife going in—

She giggled. It had been so easy. Nothing to it. Stab, stab, stab. How many times? She knew her whole arm and shoulder ached.

Now she felt anger. What a stupid thing to do. Here in the house, where she couldn't hide the body. But Dyann had time to think. Mother was with her friend in Sound Beach. Thanks for the info, June.

Dyann drank more vodka, no longer tasting it. She'd have to pack up and go. Take the train to the city. Cut her hair, dye it. She'd be with them finally. Free, finally. She knew where Mother hid extra cash.

She hurled the glass across the room. Dyann clenched her fists and shut her eyes. She had to think this out. Where the hell was Eddie, anyway? Hadn't he done it yet? How long did it take to strangle a little witch like Cara?

She lifted her head and took deep breaths. Her head screamed with pain. She'd write a goodbye note. Mother would think she'd run out before this happened. The knife was already wiped clean. She'd take it on the train, change cars, and drop it onto the tracks. They'd never know who killed June Brady.

Rising to her feet, Dyann began to feel stronger. She was out of this town, out of this life. That's why Eddie had come to her, to show her how to be free.

Now she gazed at June, almost curiously, no longer sick or frightened. She'd done something amazing. The thought made her breathe more quickly.

She gripped the banister, anxious to pack. Then she stopped as she heard a key in the front door.

Immobile, she watched as Mother came in. A gust of cold wind followed her.

Mother was cradling a sack of groceries in one arm. Dyann watched her as she noticed June. It was funny, in a way, how Mother dropped the groceries. Everything stopped at that moment while Mother screamed and screamed.

CHAPTER
19

Cara still refused to believe the truth. Any moment he would stop the truck, let her out, show her that he'd only gone around the block a few times. She'd kiss him and go back to the party. She'd cut her cake and everyone would surround her and clap.

No good. Reality was a road. He'd been driving straight and fast for so long now. He played the radio, loud. Where were they going? How far from her home?

I see Albany on a map, circled in red.

He was driving up to Albany. He'd had it circled in red, on the map she'd seen in Mr. Haller's room.

No. That was Eddie Belmonte.

She hoisted herself up by the quilting, moaning at the pain in her shoulder. Her arm throbbed under the Ace bandage, swollen, probably bleeding. She leaned against the side of the truck, looking at the back of his head through the grating.

"Danny!"

He lowered the volume. "What?"

"I have to go to the bathroom."

"Soon."

"Where are you taking me?"

"Can't say."

"What's this all about, Danny? What did I ever do to you?"

"Not to me."

"What's that supposed to mean?"

"Not important."

She slid down to the truck floor again and leaned her head back. Did June know about this? Had she gone to the police?

Slowly her denial gave way to terror. She was his prisoner. She'd always wondered how you could be kidnapped with millions of people around. But people didn't notice. Drivers on this road saw a beat-up panel truck and a redheaded kid driving. Nobody suspected there was a girl in the back.

I see the lights shatter, and then I see darkness. I feel that hatred again, but I don't see you.

The darkness was not death, but the stupid panel truck. That's why June couldn't see her. But why would Danny hate her?

Through the despair, weird thoughts blinked, like fireflies in a fog. June saw a redheaded boy in her life. Danny appeared. Cara fell in love.

How nicely it fitted.

But it didn't make sense for Danny to kidnap her, or do any of those other things. And how would he get a spider into her book bag? On one of their car rides?

Cara tried lying flat on the truck bed, but she kept sliding every time he took a curve. She could see a crack of road between the back doors. If she hurled herself against them—

Yeah, out the back of the truck at seventy miles an hour.

If she could figure out the answers, she could do something. Redheaded boy. Did Dyann know a redheaded boy? Did Dyann know Danny? Same name, anagram. Brother and sister? Cousins? Lovers? Who knew?

Anger spread through her now. She dragged herself upright again, not thinking about how much she hurt. She edged her way toward the grating, grabbed the mesh with her fingers. The wire bit into her skin.

"Danny?"

She saw his face reflected in the rearview mirror. He was wearing sunglasses. At night. "Get down."

"I need the bathroom."

"Later."

"I'll pee all over your truck."

"Go ahead."

"Why are you wearing shades at night?"

"Headlights hurt my eyes."

He cranked the volume. She felt dry wind coming through the open cab window. She hung on, as her body slammed into the panel. She glimpsed dark road through the windshield, and an exit sign, but she couldn't make out the number.

"Why are we going to Albany?" she asked.

He kept driving, but his fingers tightened on the wheel.

"Is that where you're meeting Dyann? Are you two hooked up or something?"

"Get down," he said again.

"I don't like it down there. I want to see where I'm driving." *And maybe somebody will see me.*

"You're pissing me off."

"Oh, too bad!"

He ignored her. She grimly hung on, taking heart from seeing road and light. Maybe a cop would pass, maybe Danny would get a speeding ticket, maybe she could get someone's attention. . . .

She remembered the sunglasses she'd found in the Toyota. Sort of like the ones he wore now. So Danny liked sunglasses. If only Cara had gotten them to June. Why had he picked her? Why?

Dyann hated her. Dyann took over the newspaper. Maybe Dyann and Danny planned to shake up Cara so she'd quit the paper. Okay, so Danny was Dyann's cousin from somewhere, but why this kidnapping?

There were lots of signs now, and lots of lights. They must be near Albany.

"Where are we?" she asked.

He jammed down on the brake and lurched forward again. She lost her grip on the mesh and crashed into the panel, then into the side of the truck. Pain hurled through her shoulder. Screaming, she rolled across the truck bed.

The truck slowed, turned, probably onto an exit ramp. He had to pay a toll if this was the thruway! If she could get up and scream—

He sped up. With a curse, she brought a fist down on the floor. That's why he'd thrown her down, to shut her up while he went through the toll. He drove around a long curve, and she sensed darkness. They were on a back road now.

Darkness. June had seen the darkness. Cars coming out of the darkness, spiders, knives. All of it had come true. He'd done all of it.

Cara turned her face to keep from bumping it on the floor as the truck jerked and jounced. Something was screwy about it.

Listen to me, Cara. A psychic isn't a supernatural being. Sometimes I have a mystical awareness of things, and I can sense reality from outside myself. But it's not a game, and I can't tell you for certain what will happen.

Not for certain. Not down to the exact incident. A car, a spider, a knife. But what if he *knew* what June said? If Dyann had told him? Of course. She'd spilled it all to Dyann and Thea and Nick. Dyann had told Danny, and Danny had *made* it come true.

Cara slithered to the quilting, got up a third time. She flung herself at the panel, grabbed the mesh. "She told you, right?"

He looked into the rearview mirror again. The reflection from his sunglasses unnerved Cara.

"You knew the predictions. Then you made them come true. How come? So Dyann could get revenge? You nearly killed me so Dyann wouldn't feel bad? Was that it?"

She caught a flicker of a smile. "Pretty smart."

"Yeah, but there's more, right? What else, Danny? If that's your real name. Is it? Is Danny Schonberg your real name?"

"Can't say."

Where *were* they? She saw nothing but darkness

rushing past the truck. "Probably isn't," she said. "Danny, Dyann. Dyann, Danny. You just mixed up Dyann's name to get Danny, right?"

"Yeah, right."

"And what about Schonberg? Is that made up too? Beautiful mountain. Where did you come up with beautiful . . ."

Mountain.

Monte.

Beautiful.

Bella.

Belmonte.

Oh my God.

He looked up again and light glinted from his sunglasses. "You still there?"

She slowly let her fingers slip from the grate and slid to the floor of the truck. He turned up the radio and sped through the night.

Nancy sat in Cara's living room and flipped channels, but she didn't stay with anything. Finally she came back to the local news channel. The weather report was on. She leaned back. Soon they'd get back to the story of the missing girl and the manhunt.

The house swarmed with people. Mrs. Nelson was really in bad shape. The doctor had been there and given her a sedative. Cara's brother and sister were somewhere and a couple of detectives were in the kitchen, by the phone.

Cara's sister came in and dropped down next to Nancy. "How are you doing?"

"How are *you* doing?" Nancy asked.

"Crappy. It's so insane. Why anybody would take her away—"

Andrea lost it. Nancy swallowed hard and hung on to her. The news came on again and Nancy jacked up the volume. "Still no clue as to where Cara Nelson might be. In another bizarre incident, June Brady, the psychic stabbed by a Westfield teenager, remains comatose. Police are questioning Dyann Wilson, so far without success."

Nancy shut off the TV. Next to her, Andrea wept softly. Nancy glanced at the detectives who sipped coffee and waited for a call from Danny. The only person who could find Cara was June, and June was unconscious.

Nancy leaned back and listened to the horrible sounds around her. She tried not to think of where Cara was now, or what was happening to her.

Dyann looked down at her hands. She sat in a small room at the precinct house. Detective Greene paced around her and she felt suffocated by his bulk. She wanted to go to sleep. She had a really bad hangover.

"Why did you stab her?" Detective Greene asked.

"I didn't stab her," Dyann said.

"We found the knife," he repeated. "In your drawer."

"I just keep that for protection."

Detective Greene pulled out a chair and sat down. "That knife stabbed Ms. Brady, and you held it. We took blood and skin fragments from your clothing, and they match. We want to know why she was in the house with you and why you stabbed her?"

Dyann shrugged. "I don't know."

"Yes, you do."

Dyann swallowed down the vomit. How could Mother walk in then? June told her that Mother was at a friend's house—

A lie. June had tricked her, and now she'd never get to the city.

Detective Greene leaned toward her. "Dyann, help us find your friend."

"I already helped you."

"No, Dyann. You told us Eddie Belmonte was going to kill her, but Cara's friends say it was her boyfriend who took her away."

"So find her boyfriend."

"Do you know where they might be?"

Looking up, Dyann said, "How would I know?"

"Where's Eddie right now?"

Another shrug. "I don't know."

"You do know."

Trembling, Dyann clasped her hands. "Go to hell."

Detective Greene stood up. "Sooner or later you'll tell us. If Ms. Brady dies, you're up for manslaughter."

"I don't care," she said.

"Why was Ms. Brady in your house?"

"I don't know."

"What did she tell you?"

"I wasn't listening."

With a heavy sigh, Detective Greene walked to a window and looked out. "Don't you want to rest, Dyann? It's been a tough day."

"Yes. I want to rest."

"So cooperate and you can get some sleep."

"Drop dead."

He laughed softly. "You're in for a long night."

Dyann studied the wood grain patterns on the table-top. She felt empty, as if a plug had been pulled somewhere in her back and everything had drained through the hole. She had no more puke left, no more crying, no more anger. Eddie had done this to her. He'd shown her how to be free, then deserted her. Now she'd be punished, and never see the city, or Daddy.

Chewing her lip, Dyann visualized Cara's death. Only that gave her some pleasure now.

In a hospital corridor Thea sat on a wooden bench. She kept her hands folded on her lap. Her mom was in the solarium. Nurses chattered, carts rattled. Thea heard horrible coughing.

It was good to be alone. Earlier, TV people had put on bright lights and asked her questions. She'd gotten ill. She wondered what she'd do if Aunt June died.

She thought of Dyann and could sort of see her. She was at a table somewhere. Her mind was flat. Thea remembered riding in the car with Dyann, watching the strange roads go by.

Thea looked up just then, and Aunt June's spirit touched and entered her. For an instant, Thea saw a green map with the word *Albany* circled in red. Then there was just floating again, like dark gray clouds.

Thea wondered if she ought to tell someone about the image. Not that Cara had ever been that nice to her. Not that *anybody* had ever been that nice to her.

Maybe she'd just forget about it. Nobody wanted her help anyway.

CHAPTER
20

The truck finally hissed to a stop. Cara hugged her knees in a corner, no longer caring about the time. He was Eddie Belmonte, and she'd been in love with him. How many kids in Westfield knew that Eddie Belmonte had caring blue eyes or could talk you into his heart?

Or that Eddie was sick enough to hit somebody with a car, or put spiders in your book bag, or cut you with a knife? She felt a deep, cold anger and a sense of resignation.

She heard him slam the cab door. Her heart fluttered wildly as she thought of bolting past him.

The handle turned and the door was yanked open. A flashlight blinded her. "Crawl toward me," he said.

She felt her way to the back of the truck. He grasped her wrist and jerked her out. She thudded onto soft ground, her cheek in wetness. He was straddling her, tugging back her hands. Her shoulder screamed.

She felt rope being twined around her wrists, through her fingers. He pulled it taut. Concentrating, she stretched her fingers out so she could scrunch them together later and loosen the knots.

"Why are you doing this?" she pleaded.

She felt his fingers under her arm, nudging her up. He'd turned off the headlights and she could barely make him out against blackness. Stars burned brilliantly, but there was no moon.

"Where are we?"

"Upstate."

He pushed her forward and she nearly pitched to the ground again. With a shove, he forced her against the side of the truck. She remembered kissing him, and felt dirty.

"What is this, Eddie?" she asked. "Is it some kind of stupid revenge for Dyann? Is she behind this?"

"She's one reason," he said. He opened the door of the truck cab, and reached in. "I'm another reason."

He pulled out a rifle. She strangled on her terror. "You're crazy."

"Right." He cocked the bolt and aimed the rifle at her. "I don't know how I want to do this."

She shut her eyes. Could she run tied up? How far before he shot her in the back?

He said, "Open your eyes."

She opened them. He lowered the rifle and leaned on it, like a walking stick. "Knife? It hurts. It can take a long time."

The memory of being slashed made her giddy with horror. He was going to kill her. He'd turned Dyann from a simpering wreck to a killer—and one heck of an editor. He'd convinced Cara to lose her heart and take chances. He had so much power, but he was so twisted, and so dangerous.

"Did she pay you?" Cara asked.

"Strangulation," he said. "No weapons. Could be anybody."

"It's not my fault the jocks hassled her. Killing me isn't going to make her life better."

"Yeah, it will. You never went through life getting kicked around. Watching the jocks take away the best girls. Watching hotshots like you get whatever you want."

"I never got everything," Cara said. "But I didn't run people over!" Cara twisted her wrists trying to feel if the knots were coming loose. "Did you ever kill anybody?"

Laughing, he said, "Came close with your dad."

Rage pumped through her body. "It *was* you. Why? What did he ever do to you?"

He examined the gun barrel. "Nothing. I just wanted to do it. Makes a loud bang. Didn't you ever want to do that?"

The ropes were loosening. She couldn't take the pain in her shoulder. "Everyone has crazy thoughts. Most people don't go through with them."

"That's the line," he said. "See? That's the kick. Going over the line. Chasing a couple of stupid girls in a car, any jerk can do it. Hitting one of them. Big difference."

He'd run down her dad for kicks. Run down Nancy. Put Cara through hell. He'd gone over the line, probably as a kid.

"Strangling," he said. "I want to feel it."

203

He dropped the rifle. She wriggled her hands like mad, panting at the pain. He was in front of her, staring down at her. "This is cool," he said.

His hands circled her throat. She felt her heart coming out of her chest. Wind chilled her bare shoulders. *June.*

June wasn't here.

His fingers probed her collarbone. His breath was warm on her face. Moonlight glinted from his sunglasses.

Sunglasses.

"Eddie." She could barely rasp.

"Shh," he said. His hands crawled like spiders around her throat.

"Take off the shades," she whispered.

"What"

"I want to see your eyes. Danny's eyes."

"You're as wacked as Dyann."

"Which one are you? Eddie or Danny? Huh?" This was so desperate. *You haven't lost your touch,* Nancy had told her. Mighty Mite could use an office phone during homeroom. She could wrangle June's number out of Thea. She could scam Eddie.

His laugh came low and cold. "You just want some more time."

"I don't want Eddie Belmonte to kill me. Eddie's a dork. Eddie's a class clown. I want Danny."

"Shut up."

"Come on, Danny. You're the one I love. Come on out."

"Don't you get it, you little bitch? I'm going to *kill* you."

Slowly she nudged the rope off. "You're so good at head games, but you're afraid. You're a wuss."

"Shut up!"

She wriggled her hands. They were free. "Come on, Danny. Look at me when you kill me."

For an instant he hesitated. Then he yanked off the sunglasses and flung them down. For an instant, his eyes blazed like the headlights. Every time she looked at Daddy in pain, she'd see those eyes.

"You can't do it, can you? Eddie can, but not you, Danny. You love me—"

He moaned and pushed her against the truck. *Don't think about it!* she cried silently. Swiftly, she raised her hands to his eyes and raked downward.

He shrieked. She slipped away from him. Where was the rifle? She stared around, dizzy with fear. He was cursing. He'd find her in a minute.

She saw the weapon, clawed at it two, three times, then lifted it. Heavier than she expected. Her mind begged for a decision. Not the woods; she'd get lost and he'd run her down in the truck.

Okay, the truck. She stumbled, twisting her ankle, slapped at the door in frustration.

He was coming at her. Whimpering, she found the handle, yanked downward.

She flung herself onto the front seat, dragging the rifle with her, and pulled the door shut. He screamed. Had she caught his hand? She hoped so. Oh, man, she hoped so.

He hurled himself at the truck door, again and again, until the truck began to rock. She felt along the steering wheel. He'd left the key in the ignition.

Not so brilliant, after all, but then he hadn't expected Mighty Mite to do anything.

She pumped the gas pedal and turned the key. The engine whined. He slammed into the truck again. She pumped the gas, turned the key. Lights flickered on the console. She smelled gasoline. *Don't flood out.*

The passenger window shattered and glass sprayed her. He hoisted himself up, his fingers reaching for her. Cara gripped the rifle in both hands and smashed the stock down on his knuckles. He howled and dropped away.

She pumped the pedal and turned the key. She held it and pumped again and again. The engine whined, coughed.

Caught.

A rock flew through the window, grazing her head. She raced the engine, put on the headlights, threw the truck into gear. Daddy had let her drive once or twice, teaching her the fundamentals. She'd driven illegally with friends once or twice. Not a lot of experience for a getaway.

She steered the truck over the grassy field, looking for the road. The windshield spider-webbed and she couldn't see. She stepped hard on the brake, feeling wind at her back. She realized he'd never closed the back doors. He could grab on.

She hit the gas again, not caring where she went, as long as she drove fast enough to get away from him. A rock thumped against the side of the truck.

Light blinded her, glinting along the cracks in the windshield. A deafening roar descended. That wasn't Eddie. Cara brought the truck to a jerking halt, then sat back so hard her head whiplashed against the seat.

She heard disembodied voices. Then the light moved away from the windshield and she saw a red glow. The police were there.

By the second day Cara hated her hospital room. Okay, it *was* a private room, because she was a major celebrity. Mom had brought in the newspaper with her picture on the first page. That was all incredibly cool.

But she hated hospital smells, and this was the pediatric ward so a million obnoxious little kids screamed and carried on all day and all night. She wanted to go home.

"Not yet," Mom said. "You're a mess. They need to do more tests."

As in draining her of blood. There was one nurse, the Daughter of Dracula, who kept smacking the inside of Cara's arm to find a vein. Her arm was all black and blue and hurt like blazes. No worse than her *other* arm, which had become infected, it turned out, and had to be reopened and restitched.

So Cara lay back against the now-damp pillows, not watching the TV. A teasing spring breeze drifted through the window. She looked out at cotton puff clouds and wished the nightmares would go away.

There was movement at her doorway and Cara thought, *Oh, no*, but it was Nancy, hobbling in on one crutch. "Hi," she said.

"Hi."

Nancy looked around. "I cannot *believe* this. You're *alone*."

"I know. It's amazing."

Nancy eased herself into a chair. "Well, you're old news."

"I know." Cara looked at her friend. "I really wrecked the party."

"We had fun without you. Cake was great."

"Up your nose."

"With a rubber hose," Nancy said.

"Where's Mom?"

"They dragged her away kicking and screaming."

Cara shut her eyes as the horror passed through her again. "I heard June was going to make it."

"Yeah. She's in pretty serious condition, but she'll recover."

Cara shook her head. "I can't believe Dyann did that. She was the one who *stopped* Eddie from killing me."

Nancy leaned forward and rubbed her cast. "What I heard is that she went crazy waiting for Eddie to come back and she had the knife on her and, boom, she just did it. You never know what you can do under stress."

Laughing, Cara said, "Tell me about it."

"Okay," Nancy said. "There was this time you were under stress—"

Cara yanked the pillow from behind her and flung it. Nancy ducked and the pillow knocked the plastic water pitcher off the bed table. A nurse peeked in and said, "Can we keep it down, ladies?"

Cara and Nancy tried and failed to stifle their giggling. Nancy saw Cara look over at the door and saw Mark.

Nancy gripped the sides of her chair. "I'm going, I'm going. I just can't move fast."

"No, don't get up," Mark said. He looked like a lost soul.

"Hi, Mark," Cara said.

"Hi, Caramel." He stepped into the room. "I couldn't get near here the last two days. I wanted to see how you were."

"I'm pretty good."

He looked around the room, really uncomfortable. "Look. I'm sorry about—that whole thing. I didn't know what was going on."

Nancy said, "Guys, I really think I should go."

"No, it's okay," Cara said. She hoisted herself up and demurely pulled the sheet over her wispy nightdress. "Mark, it's not your fault. I *was* cheating on you. I was scum."

"No, I was worse. Man, what I did to Dyann, it's—just stupid. I didn't think she'd lose it like that. I really feel like crap."

"You *should* feel like crap. We both should. But even though we stink, Dyann still has no excuse. You understand?"

"No," Mark said.

Cara laughed. "Mark, you are so simple. I really love you."

"Yeah, like a brother, right?"

Nancy winced. Cara said, "Naw, you're not as disgusting as my brother. But like a friend. I'm sorry. I know you hate to hear that."

He shrugged. "I figured."

"But you can come over here and kiss me. Just not too passionate. It's the kiddie ward."

He shyly made his way to the bed, and she guided his head to hers. She kissed him warmly. It felt good.

He was blushing when he straightened up. He rubbed his hair under his cap. "If they let him go, I'll be ready for him."

"Jail's definitely safer than you," Cara said. "He'll probably wind up in a funny farm."

"He's a psycho killer," Mark said angrily.

Nancy grinned. "Except he tangled with Mighty Mite." To Mark, she said, "You should be glad you never got her too upset."

"I know." He shook his head in wonderment. "You smashed his hand with a rifle butt?"

Cara leaned back, her hands over her head. "Nothin' to it."

In her mind Cara fought the horror. She needed to be happy for her friends. For herself, it would take a while. Knowing he'd hurt Daddy, remembering everything he did to her.

Nancy said, "It is just so weird how he was two people. What do you call that, paranoid?"

"Schizoid," Cara said. "But he's not schizoid. He knew who he was. He just did all that because he got a kick out of it."

"Makes no sense," Nancy said.

"I know." She imagined Mr. Haller writing today's lesson on the board: *You can't control everything.* Eddie and Dyann couldn't accept it. Cara had to learn it.

But underneath, Mr. Haller had to write: *You can control yourself.* When it got gnarly, you didn't depend on psychics. You wriggled your hands loose and did what you had to do.

"Hey, look," Nancy said.

They all looked up at the TV. It showed Dyann being taken from a car into a court building. Dyann's skin was dead white, her eyes staring.

"She should die," Mark said.

"Forget it," Cara said. "The girl is in hell, permanently."

Nancy added, "Her mom's freaking out too. Maybe she should have stayed with her dad."

"Grow up," Cara said with sudden passion. "Everything's an excuse. You don't stab people because life isn't going your way. My dad is in pain forever and he gets on with it. And look at you. You're suffering, and you're not cutting people up."

"That's because I faint at the sight of blood."

Mark laughed. Cara felt sullen. "Okay, forget it."

"Excuse *me*," Nancy said. "Just so you know, the world isn't going to end because of *your* suffering, either."

The words stung. "I was a snot."

"Definitely."

Cara leaned back, feeling sleep crawl over her. It felt good having Nancy with her, and Mark. It was good knowing Mom and Dad waited, with promises of a new TV and VCR and anything else she could wring out of them. Even another sweet sixteen party, they said. If she wanted it.

Yeah, she did. With no unexpected boyfriends.

About the Author

Richard Posner graduated from Hofstra University and holds an M.S. in education from Dowling College and an M.A. in English Literature from Queens College. He teaches English, creative writing, and journalism at Sachem High School and freshman composition at Suffolk Community College.

He has written many books for young adults and adults, and considers young adult writing to be the most rewarding: "I love being with kids, teaching them, and writing about and for them. In fact, I find many of them to be more interesting than adults."

Richard has three children. He lives with his wife on Long Island in New York, where he is at work on his next novel. His suspense novels for young adults, *Someone to Die For* and *Sweet Sixteen and Never Been Killed,* are both available from Archway Paperbacks.